THE COIN FLIP

Elizabeth Smith

ENDORSEMENTS

"This spell-bounding narrative almost seems to be too good to be true. However, the faith, determination and circumstances of this novel help us to undoubtedly see God's providence through the twists and turns of life."

- Fr. Steven Roth, Director of Vocations,
Archdiocese of Baltimore

"Libby Smith's book, The Coin Flip, is an easy, engaging read. You immediately are absorbed into the story. It was difficult for me to put it down. The dialogue makes you feel part of the story. You will enjoy this book."

- Cantor Nancy Ginsberg, Manager of Pastoral Services,
Oak Crest Senior Living

"The Coin Flip is a moving and powerful story of one man's journey as he moves to the United States to pursue his dream of becoming a priest. The unexpected twists and turns of life test young Joe Quigley's trust in God, but reveal a life more blessed than he could have imagined."

- Kathy Schmitt, MDiv.,Pastoral Administrator,
Oak Crest Catholic Community

"Libby Smith draws on her strong Catholic faith and family history to bring this tale to life. Based on true events, The Coin Flip is an inspiring tale sure to enrich your faith in God's promise. Highly recommended."

– Rev. James M. Reusing, Pastor & Spiritual Director

Although this book is a work of fiction, it draws inspiration from real-life events.

Printed and manufactured in
the United States of America

Web: www.TheCoinFlipBook.com
Email: libbygibbonssmith@gmail.com

Edited by
Michele Chynoweth

Book Composition by
Gary Adornato

Library of Congress Control Number: 2023910057

ISBN: 979-8-218-23913-8

DEDICATION

I dedicate this story to my beloved husband Dennis.

ACKNOWLEDGMENTS

I give thanks to all my family and friends for their very kind support. In particular, I appreciate Barbara Chelton, Allan Bowers and author Mark Newhouse for acting like Beta readers, my dear friend, Kathy Blake, for her artistic ideas for the cover, my book coach, editor, and friend, Michele Chynoweth, who got the ball rolling when she offered a writing class online, and my cousins, Patti Van Buskirk and Tommy Conlon, who supplied me with an old article and specific information regarding our great-grandfather which then inspired me to write this book.

I extend much gratitude to Pam Green and our whole Capital Christian Writer's Fellowship group who generously suggested ways of improvement and gave ongoing encouragement, as well as my son-in-law, Gary Adornato, who deserves credit with getting this project off the ground, and my precious, tech-savvy husband, Dennis, who patiently and calmly rescued me every time I became frantic and stressed about having trouble with the computer.

ABOUT THE AUTHOR

Elizabeth Smith, who goes by Libby, lives in Parkville, Maryland with her husband Dennis. Her previous book, *Twin Strokes*, is about a young girl who suffered with a rare illness called Guillain-Barre Syndrome.

Smith, who enjoys writing children's stories, senior jokes, articles and essays, has three children and two grandchildren. Her hobbies include, reading, writing, baking, walking, swimming, and listening to a variety of music. Among her favorite authors are; Jan Karon, Adriana Trigiani, Max Lucado, and the late, Erma Bomback. While growing up in the country, a treasured time during the summer was hiking to the nearby bookmobile.

"I have fond memories of walking inside and smelling the fragrance of the books and slowly feeling the crinkly plastic covers like they were gold," said Smith. "It was intoxicating."

Smith also enjoyed teaching Faith Formation to school children, working for a pediatrician and helping kids as a paraeducator. Eventually, she was inspired to write a middle grade novel about a young girl stricken with Guillain-Barre Syndrome. A few years later, after reading an article about her great-grandfather, it became her mission to write this book.

"I feel the Holy Spirit was my co-author in both works," added Smith.

Table of Contents

CHAPTER 1

In 1857, I slowly approached the massive, muddy brown ship with seven sails that was to take me to Liverpool, England. From there I would transfer onto a British steamship in order to travel on a long, long journey to America. With the sun shining and the breeze blowing through my hair, it seemed to be a perfect sailing day. Summer always was my favorite season. Standing amongst hundreds of people and feeling my stomach churn, I just felt lucky to be hugging the side of the vessel. There I stared at my beautiful green Irish countryside. Inhaling the fragrant air and aromatic soil, I clutched the rosary in my pocket. It was my travel gift from Ma.

Happy memories flooded my mind as I savored favorite

thoughts of family dinners and school buddies. However, I knew I was ready to explore a new country across the Atlantic. It had monopolized my dreams for the past five years.

A few happy tears trickled down my cheeks when I recalled working in the fields and on the farm. Now, it drew smiles—but then, it often brought exhaustion. "Laborious work builds character," my Pa would say. He was a mighty hard worker and such a cheerful, dependable man.

Both my Ma and Pa came from good stock. Ma would always make time for others, no matter how busy she was. She had a heart of gold. I remember her telling us, "If you can't say something nice about someone, don't say anything at all."

My aunts and uncles told me that not only did I resemble Pa in appearance, but in character too. With his tall, slim stature and dark brown hair, they even joked about our duplicate right cheek dimple, which seemed uncanny. I didn't always see it. They said at one of our family reunions that because of my excelled studies at school and reliable help on the farm, I showed responsibility and made them proud. I hope I can live up to their remarks.

They didn't realize that many times I inwardly griped about the long hours spent helping Pa. I would much rather have been playing my fiddle or whittling. I know the work was necessary, so I got angry at myself for complaining. My older brother and best friend, Aiden, was better than me. He wasn't impatient like I was.

At seventeen years old, I waved goodbye to my family. I was glad they couldn't see my puffy, red eyes. Hearing some cows mooing in the distance, I thought they too were saying goodbye. Sighing heavily, I knew in my heart that embarking on this new chapter of my life would soon work out if I kept trusting in the Lord.

Arriving in the port of Liverpool, England, was an exciting adventure. I was amazed to see numerous ships docked in the harbor. Coming from Cork, a rural town in Southwest Ireland, this scenery was new and fascinating. Various factories—where candles, matches, metal, and paper were made towered in the background expelling exhaust fumes that made me gag. Grime and soot circled the air in clouds of gray smoke. The clanging noises from these structures resonated loudly, paining my ears. I thought the sailing ship I just exited was large, but the three-master steamer I saw in front of me was enormous in comparison. I had two hours to wait before departure, so I strolled around the nearby streets hoping to distance myself from the nauseating odors.

Noticing people all around, they seemed preoccupied, not so friendly like in my hometown. In my village, when people passed each other, they would seem genuinely glad to see you and stop to chat.

On my walk I saw a poor-looking chap selling his artwork on the far end of the waterfront. Viewing all his wares, I found a picture I would have liked to buy for Ma. It was a portrait of a yellow and orange flower garden in the round that swarmed with butterflies and bumblebees. The artist even included three little robins on the ground by the flowers, pecking at some fallen seeds. I wanted so much to purchase that picture but did not have enough money. I knew I needed to save all that I brought with me for when I landed in America. Shaking my head "no" with my lips pressed tightly, the artist saw I was disappointed, as I'm sure he was too.

I still had a little time left to sightsee, so I meandered across the cobblestone street. Walking felt good after being on a crowded ship. There was a small black and white dog a few feet ahead of me who was by himself. He limped with a bandage around his left back leg. Squatting down, I petted the dog and his tail immediately wagged. I felt sorry for the seemingly forlorn animal. He licked my face and I curled him in my arms. Just then, a young boy spotted me holding his pet. He came over and claimed him and said he'd lost Cocoa in the crowd of people. He said, "Thank you, Mister, for finding my dog." I suddenly felt grown up in that moment.

Thinking it was about time to depart, I walked back to the dock only to realize we still had another half hour before departure. I was feeling impatient to leave. *The barn smells better than this,* I thought. While fanning myself, I gazed all around, fidgeting with my shirt. *Come on, let's get moving.* As if the captain could hear my thoughts, we were finally beckoned aboard. Finally, my transatlantic trip was starting. *Off to a new beginning!*

CHAPTER 2

Living on a wooden steamship with two masts for six weeks was more difficult than I could have ever imagined. I had no idea how challenging it would be. I was grateful that I was not claustrophobic. My tiny cabin was on the second level of the ship. It felt no larger than our cow stalls back home. The bed, half-broken chair, and dwarf dresser were all touching each other. I knew not to complain though because the several hundred poor souls on the lower level, which was sometimes referred to as the steerage, were clustered all together with no privacy at all. The top level consisted of the staff.

The food didn't compare to Ma's cooking, especially her warm and wholesome soda bread, and it seemed I was seasick more often than not. Most people were courteous, but I was lonely and felt isolated, even though I was surrounded by hundreds of other passengers on the bulky ship filled with piercing noises.

Our captain, Mr. Ellington, was a likeable fellow, unlike some other captains who I later heard were grumpy. This man looked rather distinguished with his short, manicured beard. His uniform was always meticulously clean. His hazel eyes drew attention to the green and bronze medal pinned to his lapel.

"How did you earn your medal, Captain?" I once in-quired, noticing its shine.

He hemmed and hauled before humbly answering me. "Well son, one day I went down to the steerage, and I noticed a little girl who was panicking. I grabbed her up and out from the middle of a cluster of insensitive people who didn't realize they knocked her over and almost trampled her. I returned her to her mother who was nursing the child's sibling about five yards away. Children can easily become distant from parents on a ship because of its overcrowded condition."

The captain then informed me that we were lucky to be traveling in the post-famine era because sanitation and medical care were a bit better now. He even showed me the making of our steamship one afternoon when he was in a jolly mood. It was constructed of wood and propelled by paddles.

"Sir, what is the purpose of the two masts?" I asked him.

"Good question. They support the wireless telegraph antennas and carry the home country flag, and since they are tall, they carry extra lighting for protection from possible accidents."

He also introduced me to a few of the shippers. Some of the men had broad smiles above their bushy beards, which were long and wiry. One man was missing two top teeth. Others had hard expressions and muttered under their breath, which indicated to me they felt rather resentful, but they all seemed to follow the captain's orders, regardless of whether or not they agreed with them.

Two weeks into my travel I met a cheerful bright young chap with curly red hair named Jim McDermott. He was eighteen, a year older than me, but we shared the same interests. Getting to know him, I finally realized I had found a friend and began to relax onboard for the first time. We passed the time playing jacks and marbles and sharing stories of our childhood adventures.

McDermott told me about his elderly neighbor who owned two enormous cherry trees. He said he would visit the old man and indulge in his juicy, plump fruit while listening to his entertaining stories interspersed with the spitting of tobacco.

McDermott told me he often expressed his joy by writing ballads and that he won a few contests at school. He said he also liked a certain lassie, but the feeling wasn't mutual. As he told me his disappointing love story, a large black bird flew overhead and gifted me in my hair. My new friend laughed heartily at that, slapping his brown suspendered trousers.

As the sun shone above us, warming our freckled Irish skin, we continued exchanging stories. I explained my job of having to pluck chicken feathers by holding a bird up by its feet after Pa wrung its neck so Ma could cook it for supper. One vicious rooster lost his life when he attacked me one too many times as I entered the coop. I lost my patience and clobbered him with a board sitting by the fence. Pa was furious! I had no dinner that night.

McDermott nodded, his ginger-colored curls bobbing under his herringbone Irish flat cap, and giggled over that, remembering a similar story. He said that once he forgot to close the chicken coop gate at night when he collected eggs. The next day he noticed three of the chickens laid dead because of a hungry fox. His father was not pleased about that either.

I told him about one scary day when my youngest brother, Patrick, was chased by a mean bull. Our faithful retriever noticed the danger and immediately distracted the bull, saving Patrick's life.

I confessed to my new friend, Jim, although we called each other by our surnames, once I cheated on a test at school. I had fearfully explained to my stern teacher Ma had a fever and I needed to take care of my three younger brothers while she rested, which resulted in less time for me to study. I could tell she knew I was truthful when her austere gaze melted away. She answered with kind words which told me she understood. However, I still had to write two hundred times, "I must not cheat."

McDermott asked me if we had cows on our farm. That led to more stories about my experiences on our land. I told him about sitting on our homemade stool while milking Lady, our old Guernsey, and how I would always dream about becoming a priest. "My dream would also be foremost in my mind when digging up the peat from the field to use for fuel to heat our home. In fact, it seemed this desire always popped into my head when doing chores. As much as I liked animals and farm life, I knew in my soul I wanted to become a priest, and the freedom of faith permitted in America was why I chose to relocate there."

"Well, well… you would never guess Quigley, that I too have the same desire!" McDermott looked at me directly, his startling yet sincere blue eyes sparkling.

"No kidding!" I gasped. "Have you known for a long time too?"

"Ever since I was an altar boy. Father Kelly inspired me when I served Mass with him for three years. He was so funny. Hc made me laugh every day. I also noticed how devoted he was to the Blessed Mother."

As we reminisced, I told him about my encouragement. "My grandpa's parish priest, Father Rich, as he was known, was one of the kindest men on earth. After working all day, he filled his wagon at night with his own food and took it to different needy families several nights a week. Then he stayed a spell to visit and pray with them. He told Grandpa that sometimes he was so exhausted he almost fell asleep riding home. Luckily, his horse knew the way."

"Well, I hope we can fare as well as they did," said McDermott.

Just then, a youngster bumped up against my hip while running with his friend. He made me think of my younger brothers, whom I missed dreadfully.

I asked McDermott if he had any siblings. "Yeah, I have two sisters and one brother. My one sister just left for the convent this year following in our aunt's footsteps. My other sister got married three years ago to a good chap. My brother is a fisherman. I am the youngest in our family. How about you, Quigley?"

"I have four brothers—one older, working on our farm, and three younger ones still in elementary school. We all used to enjoy fishing together when chores were over. Sometimes when we capered down our narrow road, I felt rascally and would trip one or the other and they would fall into a cow patty. Other times we would cozy up under a maple tree and read our favorite books. When I was in a musical mood, which was most of the time, I played my fiddle that my grandfather gave me. We all headed out to the pasture and had fun jigging around for a while."

"Do you play an instrument, McDermott?"

"I like the tin whistle and I would join my brother with his Bodhran drum when he had time. Music raises the heart to higher heights, doesn't it?"

"Sure does," I agreed, recalling how oftentimes on Sundays, relatives would congregate at our cottage while my two cousins joined me by playing their mandolins. Then Ma would fix us a hearty, delicious dinner of colcannon and sausage, and of course, her soda bread. *Good memories.*

"Quigley," he said, "you know it will take lots of money to be educated for the priesthood, right?" Pondering McDermott's words, I nodded in somber agreement. After thinking for a few minutes about how we would possibly pay for our education, it began to rain. We decided to retire to our quarters and discuss it later.

I really like that chap McDermott. He seems genuine and sounds determined and focused.

Lying across my musty, smelly bed with ragged sheets, anxiety began to surface.

I couldn't stop thinking about our financial dilemma. *Somehow it has to happen. I will come up with the money. I cannot let a lack of funds ruin my dream.* My head pounded from the thought.

CHAPTER 3

I woke up, startled by a scream outside of my room. As I flung open my door, some shippers were running down to the lower deck. Someone yelled from below that a crowd of men were in a big brawl, so I went down to see the commotion. Blood was everywhere. One of the men yelled about his broken arm. One had gotten slammed onto the floor. Another one had his spectacles broken. Another wrestler knocked his enemy unconscious. Two men had black eyes and swollen faces. It was a horrible mess.

The shippers, who acted like the Garda back home, tried to break up the fight between the steerage passengers. After much effort they were able to pull the fighters apart. The quarrel ended with the men being thrown into solitary cells for three days. I heard later it had all started when someone had made some cruel wisecracks to the others.

I headed back to my room and decided to rummage through my trunk for something to pass the time. Even though I was bored, I was still glad I had at least been able to afford quarters on the second floor of the steerage. Under my clothing lay my Bible and fiddle. Trying to calm myself, I plucked the strings. I then heard a knock at my door. McDermott came in and smiled, telling me he enjoyed what he heard.

"How about if I get my tin whistle and join you in some fun?"

"Fine with me."

After an hour, we decided we better go to the dining area before we missed supper. Trying to appreciate a dry, rather hard biscuit and small piece of trout, I imagined what my family was eating. I could almost taste Ma's spicy lamb along-side her thick-sliced tomatoes, cubed potatoes and onions sizzling in our old heirloom frying pan. *Now that was a meal.*

We shuffled back to my room. I fell back onto my bed while McDermott slumped into my so-called chair. It was tilted to the right which made him fall. Trying again, he spread his legs to balance himself. We decided to read the Bible, even though the catechism was more often our book of study in class. When we closed the book of Psalms, I spoke to McDermott about our vocations.

"It's going to take us a long time to come up with the money for our education," I said, feeling anxious again. "We will need to maybe work in a shipyard or do bookkeeping for quite a while before we save enough money."

McDermott noticed me wringing my hands and biting my lip. "Quigley, don't be so worried. We'll think of something."

He said this as he walked confidently out of my room, humming "Amazing Grace."

I wished I could be so sure.

I had a long night's sleep, a better one than usual. I remembered dreaming about my grandfather. He told me some of his amusing stories around our hearth. I was the only one with him at the time in my dream. He played a little ditty on his fiddle that seemed to go along with each story. The end of my dream was from a real-life experience when he offered me his instrument a week before his death. I could not have been more honored. When I woke up the next morning, the dream was so heavy on my mind that I played his fiddle for about twenty minutes, feeling deeply nostalgic.

Later in the morning a storm began brewing. Within a short time, turbulent winds started alarming the passengers. The crew walked around the ship ordering everyone to take precaution by evacuating the deck and returning to their rooms. McDermott decided to keep company with me instead of heading to his own room.

Lightning exploded as bright as fireworks. Rain thrashed hard and heavy over our vessel. A woman screamed when water burst through her cabin door. McDermott and I darted out to the rocking walkway and tried to console her. It took a while to calm the frantic, elderly woman. She bunked with a relative until her room was clear of the water. We heard some whimpering from the frightened children following the many thunder clashes. The storm was wicked for most of that day.

By evening, the brutal rainstorm subsided. McDermott and I decided to venture out onto the quarterdeck to see the ocean. Off in the distance, seagulls flew and a school of dolphins gracefully glided across the waves, apparently indifferent to the sea's disturbance. Breathing deeply, I inhaled the fresh, cool air which felt invigorating after so many days of sultry summer heat. Staring up at the moon, which shyly peeked out from behind a cloud, a peaceful feeling swept over my previous inner turmoil and allayed my ongoing financial fears.

I knew I had to work at trusting God, becoming more patient and less anxious, and in this moment, once again I believed that somehow, in His way and time, everything would work out. *Wouldn't it?*

The Coin Flip

CHAPTER 4

The next day, as I walked the deck, Captain Ellingham waved hello. He stopped to talk.

“Would you and your buddy like to check out our compass and telescope? I can show you tomorrow morning if you come to my cabin.”

. “We’ll be there, thanks!”

“What are your plans for traveling to America, son? Do you intend to visit relatives or move there?”

“I hope to work for a while to earn enough money for schooling. I would like to be a priest.”

“Well, I hear there are plenty of opportunities in the factories and on the railroad."

"Thanks Captain, I appreciate that information, but I think I am more suited as a bookkeeper while I study for the priesthood." *Maybe, I can work and attend classes at the same time.*

"Your choice, son. I better get back to the wheel before we head in the wrong direction." His deep-set eyes twinkled in his worn, weather-beaten face as he chuckled.

I said goodbye, wondering about my uncertain future, and headed to my cabin. I felt nervous again and my patience was wearing thin, but I knew I needed to try to relax and see what was offered when I arrived in America. *I know God will have something for me, but I'm not giving up my dream of enrolling in the seminary.*

When I turned the corner of the deck to head downstairs to my quarters, McDermott approached me. I mentioned what the captain said about seeing his compass and telescope tomorrow. He whistled with excitement.

"The captain mentioned to me about railroad and factory jobs in America, too."

"Speaking of that," McDermott said, "let's talk about what jobs might pay the most money so it doesn't take us so long to enter the seminary."

"I don't think we will know until we arrive in America and investigate it."

"True, but I don't feel like waiting ten years to enter."

"Neither do I."

There was a long pause. Suddenly, McDermott squealed and jumped into the air, snapping his fingers.

"I got it, Quigley! How about if we flip a coin? The loser will get a job and pay the winner to go to the seminary? That way, at least one of us can afford to become a priest right away."

"I don't know, McDermott." I answered with trepidation, rubbing the back of my neck. "That's going to be hard for the loser."

"Well, my word is good, Quigley. And who knows, maybe after a few years the loser will have saved enough for himself to enter seminary too?"

Stalling, I turned away. "Not sure I agree."

"It's the only way we can manage to help each other with our same goal. One priest is better than none."

My chest tightened and I felt tense all over. "Maybe, but let's pray about it first," I answered hesitantly.

"Sure, good idea," he replied.

We decided to return to my room and pray the Rosary."

I opened my only cabinet drawer and pulled out the blue crystal rosary that Ma gave me. McDermott had a deep red one given to him at his Confirmation in his pants pocket. We began the Sorrowful Mysteries, alternating each decade. In the middle of praying, I started feeling an inner peace flowing through me. I knew God and the Blessed Mother Mary were hearing our plea for advice.

We finished praying the Rosary. "I suppose I'm ready for the toss…as ready as I'll ever be." I inhaled and held my breath.

"Ok, who calls first?" McDermott asked.

"I don't care," I answered, my heart thudding rapidly in my chest.

He handed me his shilling. "Call."

I called heads. Up in the air the coin went. Landing on the bare wooden floor, the coin stopped spinning. Tails appeared. We broke eye contact as I lowered my head. *Oh dear God, I don't believe what just happened. How can it be?*

"You win," I answered with a defeated smile, trying to seem like a good sport. I had never felt more disappointed in my entire life. My dream had just collapsed in an instant. I sighed, heartbroken. "Well, I will certainly keep true to our bargain," I said, forcing myself to sound cheerful. "No worry there. You can trust me, Jim. When we dock in New York, you can head right to St. Monica's Church and sign up and I will begin investigating the best paying job."

We settled our deal with a firm handshake.

It took hours before I fell asleep that night. I was in a complete daze and whispered to God, "What is your plan for me Lord, if not to be a priest?" Confusion swam through my head. I felt totally puzzled, sad, and frustrated. My whole life was heading in a different direction. *What was my purpose now? Why didn't I win? I don't believe this happened! I thought that's what You wanted too God?*

CHAPTER 5

The following morning McDermott and I traipsed over to the captain's station for our tour. I followed blindly, still feeling shocked from the outcome of our toss. *Why did I lose?*

Captain Ellington greeted us with a cigarette hanging from the side of his mouth. "Good day, lads. Glad to show off the running of this vessel. I had a boy about your age before he had a fatal accident. Sea life was in his bones. I had high hopes of him taking over my ship, but it wasn't meant to be."

"May I ask what happened to him, sir?," asked McDermott

"Yes, son. One day he was out with his buddy for a joy-ride. During an unexpected storm, they lost all steerage due to a mechanical failure. While they tried to repair it, a wooden beam fell on top of my son's head. It knocked him out cold. His friend, near dead himself from exhaustion, finally came into port many hours later. The doctor pronounced my boy dead and said it looked to him like death came immediately. At least he didn't lay suffering." The captain exhaled a shallow sigh. "My nephew has no desire to be on the water. He prefers factory work. So now, let's get started. Your names?"

"I am Joe Quigley."

"Mine is Jim McDermott."

"Over to your right is our prized binnacle given to me as a gift from my Pa, George Ellington. There was no better sea captain in all of England. Nice and shiny she is. Yes, siree. They don't come any prettier. I have one of our shippers polish her every month. She holds our magnetic compass which detects the northward direction."

"That compass looks heavy," I said, circling the binnacle.

"Yes, it is thirty-five pounds. We have a backup one if needed, but so far this works just fine." The captain pointed to a gray case behind me and said it was his telescope. "You boys can look through it if you want."

Bending down to look through the instrument, McDermott replied, "Wow, amazing! I sure never needed this on the farm."

"Now, for the main job of navigation, we have our ten-spoke steering wheel. Some ships have eight spokes, but I prefer ten. It comes as high as your neck, Joe."

"Yes sir, it sure does," I said indifferently with tightened hands in my pocket. I could barely talk I was so preoccupied with the result of yesterday's toss.

"What's the diameter of this wheel?' McDermott asked curiously.

"Sixty inches, a good size. I bet you fellows could run this ship if necessary."

"I wouldn't like to be tested," McDermott answered as he stepped slightly back.

While they were talking, I felt fatigued. My head pounded. I did not want to be there at all. In a weak tone of voice, I thanked Captain Ellington and excused myself, admitting I didn't feel well. He told me there was a doctor on board if I cared to see him, and Jim said he'd catch up with me later.

They continued conversing while I shuffled back to my bed. I laid down and wanted to sleep forever. *Why, God, did I lose? I thought it was my vocation to be a priest? What do you want me to do now? Please show me because I sure don't know. Maybe after making enough money for McDermott, I can save for myself. Just tell me God, what should I do?* Then a familiar Bible quote came to me. *"Your ways, O Lord, make known to me; teach me your paths."* I prayed myself to sleep.

Upon waking a few hours later, I played my fiddle. It seemed to be my saving grace.

Later at supper, McDermott related to me the news

about the escaped bird. One of the passengers had brought along his cockatiel. Apparently the cage lock broke open, which gave the bird free reign of the ship. It caused a lot of commotion flying and squawking all over the decks. The children were entertained all afternoon. The bird perched itself on peoplcs' heads, on their laps, essentially anywhere it pleased. McDermott said it was so funny to watch. Some man finally caught the bird as it stationed itself on his wife's shoulder. "You missed a good show, Quigley," McDermott said laughing.

Back in my room, I sat listlessly on my bed after supper. I spied a small envelope that was sticking up on the side of my trunk. *What is this?* I perked up with curiosity. I hungrily ripped it opened and my heart instantly smiled as I recognized Aiden's penmanship…

"Dear Joe, know that we all miss you, brother. However, we are glad you are able to pursue your life dream. How do you like the steamboat journey? When you write back, tell us all about it. You confided in me that you are trying to overcome your impatience. Therefore, I thought I would just give

you a little reminder, although I'm sure you are aware of it. I too am trying to change a bad habit. You know mine is cursing as we have discussed. I had to bite my lip the other day when I was ready to curse up a storm seeing the calves escaping from a broken fence. I look forward to hearing from you when you arrive in America and settle into your new place. Enclosed is an extra copy of St. Patrick's prayer that I had. Stay well, Joe. Your best friend and brother, Aiden."

Clutching the letter to my chest, I sighed. *Oh Aiden, you have no idea*, I said silently with regret. *I was so impatient to figure everything out that I carelessly tossed away my dream, the one I left home for, in a matter of seconds...in the flip of a coin. You don't know how devastated I feel. Completely lost. How can life change so abruptly? I don't understand, I just don't. I feel angry, too.* Punching my pillow, I growled through clenched teeth.

A heavy knock came at my door. "Someone's cigarette fell on a nearby rag and a fire broke out over the back side of the bottom deck!" McDermott yelled. He told me to come out quick, that people were screaming, and some were badly hurt and needed help.

We ran down the stairs, dodging fleeing men, women, and children, almost tripping over the last few steps. People cried hysterically in the hallway. We edged ourselves toward the fire along with several middle-aged passengers and some shippers. What a frightful sight! A few people had burn marks on their arms and faces. Others were passed out from the fumes. Ashes flew all over the area. One man saw us and pointed to a poor soul gasping for breath. We carried him up to a top deck where he could get some air. When his breathing settled, we scurried down the steps to help the others.

We saw an elderly man lying on his side, looking at us desperately. As McDermott and I approached him, we noticed that the man was dying. With widened eyes, we stared at each other and knew we needed to immediately pray for him. Kneeling by his side, we began praying and interceding for this stranger. Gently moving him out of the crowd, we found a bench and laid him down. I removed my shirt and placed it over the man.

We then found the captain and reported the fire to him. Fortunately, the crew worked fast to extinguish the flames. After a short time, the horrific episode ended. McDermott and I admitted that we never had to experience a fire on our farms, thank the Lord.

Emotionally exhausted, we retreated to my room and played music together. When we finished, I showed him my small whittling knife and piece of cedar. When he tried his hand at this new skill, a lighthearted feeling came over both of us and we began joking.

"You'll have this down in no time," I told him. "You can give a demonstration in your parish and show off your art-work. By then, this fish that you're trying to carve will actually look like one and not like a mouse." I teased him, trying not to be jealous.

I should just be grateful I wasn't hurt in the fire, I reprimanded myself. Still…my heart ached despite my display of gaiety.

CHAPTER 6

The next day, feeling restless, I decided to station myself on the upper deck for hours. I needed to smell the salty air, enjoy the blazing sun, and attempt to renew my broken spirit. Of course, with so many people on the ship, I had a hard time finding privacy.

I finally saw a vacant spot at the edge of the bow, large enough for me to look out and think. Inhaling the fresh sea air was intoxicating. Squinting at the mighty sun, I turned my head around to the right. I was astounded to see several whales. I could not believe my eyes. The creatures were enormous. It looked like they were spouting water up in the air. *Amazing!* The sounds they made were heavy and deep. I was totally mesmerized. I hardly felt the choppy water splashing me.

My whale watching lasted awhile until I got distracted by some beautiful birds that I later discovered were called "blue herons." They made their appearance by hovering over the ship, gliding effortlessly along, and then diving down into the water for fish. It was another magnificent new sight for me and suddenly the fear and doubt that had weighed me down turned into joy and praise for the Creator that had made it all.

That led me into personal and heartfelt prayer about my turmoil. *Lord God, I am trying so hard to accept this change that has happened to me. I know it's for a reason and I may or may not find out why. Please let me be able to discern Your will and know Your direction with joy. I love You. Glory be to the Father, and the Son, and the Holy Spirit, as it was in the beginning, is now and ever shall be, world without end, Amen.*

A wave of contentment rolled over me as I watched the ocean waves whirl. My mind traveled back to Ireland, and I wondered how my family was doing. Since it was mid-afternoon, I knew milking time was approaching. The boys were probably playing in the hay or gathering the garden vegetables for dinner. Aiden was no doubt plowing the far pasture.

I should have thought to park myself at this spot weeks ago. It filled me with peace. Now with only one day left on this journey, I had to mentally prepare myself for what I would be facing when I arrived in New York.

At dinner, we were told to gather our belongings together because we were going to dock in New York early the next morning before dawn. What a relief it would be to have no more sea sickness. McDermott and I planned to meet each other shortly before sunrise. My journey across the great Atlantic was coming to an end. *Would I ever return to my homeland?* I wondered.

Hundreds of people crowded on deck, ready to exit the ship the following day. A few babies cried and some children squabbled while parents led them forward, but everyone followed the directions that were yelled over both ends of the ship. It was a little chaotic to say the least.

The Coin Flip

I got chills as I gazed straight ahead at the round brick building that stood as a welcoming site for immigrants in the New York harbor. One of the other passengers told me that it was called Castle Garden, and that previously it was a theatre and dining house. Prior to that, it was a military fort. I was completely awestruck and said a prayer of thanksgiving for a safe arrival. The damp, cloudy weather did not distract me from the sight of my awaited destination. I felt glad to exit from the fishy smell of the harbor and the deafening sound of ship bells coming into port. Many hours later, feeling nearly breathless, I walked gingerly on the newfound soil I would soon call home. Straight ahead were American flags atop all the buildings fluttering in the breeze as if they were welcoming us to their hospitable dwelling.

Dealing with mixed feelings of fear and excitement coupled with fatigue, I stood in line with everyone else for what seemed like days on end. There were rows and rows of us immigrants waiting to be registered. In the inspection hall we had to have a medical check to make sure we weren't contagious with any disease. Our documents were also checked so they could verify our identities. Going through customs took so long, I felt I was ready to scream. It was grueling and I started to question why I'd ever embarked on this journey in the first place.

It was then I recalled Aiden's kind reminder of staying calm and patient. Psalm 138:8 popped into my head. *"The Lord will work out his plans for my life—for your loving kindness, Lord, continues forever."*

I was able to smile again when I saw McDermott five people ahead of me. We waved at each other and nodded. We had previously decided to meet after leaving the inspection hall.

When the customs ordeal finally ended, we found each other again and waited some more to hail a crowded ferry which we boarded and took to the mainland.

At last we arrived, breathing in the humid New York City air. What a bustling place! Factories and shops were in view everywhere we turned. The noises were deafening.

Locals were shoulder to shoulder, heading in all directions, some knocking into us as we meandered along the concrete sidewalks and asphalt streets. My stony impression of this new environment was shared by my friend. We felt rather shocked. I instantly felt homesick. *Why am I here, especially after losing my dream?* I wondered with dismay. *I want to turn back right now.* I was feeling resentful. We tried to orient ourselves in our confusion. Rubbing my chin, I told McDermott we needed to first find a pub and have a decent meal, one better than those on the ship. Someone walking toward us gave us a good suggestion.

After eating a satisfying plate of beef stew and drinking a pot of strong tea at a local Irish eating house, we felt refreshed and able to carry on.

CHAPTER 7

McDermott and I next sought out St. Monica's Catholic Church. It was constructed with an impressive stucco exterior located on Fifth Avenue in Manhattan. This large church was bigger than any back home. It was the one Archbishop Kearney told us to go to in his letter when we arrived. We were told we could stay temporarily until we found a permanent home in the seminary. St. Patrick's Cathedral was beginning to be built but was only partially constructed. I later learned it took twenty-two years for it to be completed.

We walked over to the rectory and knocked on the door. Archbishop Kearney welcomed us with open arms. His sunken violet-blue eyes shone with kindness and his grayish hair spoke of his aging years. The black cleric could not conceal his stocky middle.

We stayed for two hours, telling the archbishop about our experiences on the steamship. He gave us a tour of the Church of St. Monica and we remarked how much newer and nicer it looked than our humbler parishes back home. Then we explained about our coin toss.

"Oh Joe, I feel terribly sorry," the old pastor said, kindly laying his wrinkled hand on my shoulder. "I know you must be heartbroken. God has His reasons for what happens during our life's journey, and we may not find out why until we reach heaven. We just need to trust that it is somehow for our good or the good of others."

"Yeah," I answered despondently. "It sure is tough though."

"Of course it is."

He paused and then added, "I remember one year as a kid I wanted to ride our tractor and my father said no, I was too young and might get hurt. I was angry. Later that day when he drove it, one of the back wheels came loose and jerked him off. He was able to catch himself, but I would have been thrown and injured. I know that is a poor comparison, but I'm just trying to make you feel better and hopefully help you to understand."

The archbishop sensed how sad I felt and said I was welcome to reside in one of his guest rooms until I got settled with a job and place to stay. That sounded mighty good to me. McDermott was only planning to stay overnight and then head to the seminary.

"I guess I will acquire a position somewhere in the city," I told McDermott and the archbishop. "I do have a knack for numbers, so I'm going to try bookkeeping."

"Good for you, Quigley," McDermott said, smiling sheepishly, his cheeks flushed pink. "I'm glad you decided what you're going to be doing. I'm sure you'll make a fine accountant. I admit I feel a little guilty though."

"Don't feel guilty McDermott. You won, fair and square."

Archbishop Kearney explained to him where to find the seminary. "Jim, it's a brand new structure, just finished a few months ago. You will need to take the train because it's located about three hundred miles west of here in Allegany, New York. I have the train schedule in my desk drawer to give to you. I hear it is a beautiful stone building with outdoor stations bordering a woodsy path and named Christ the King Seminary. It's located a few miles from the station, in a serene setting, so you will need to take a carriage ride from the train."

"Many thanks, Archbishop. I have a good amount of traveling ahead of me so I must excuse myself, say goodnight to you both, and hit the hay. I will check the schedule first thing in the morning."

McDermott and I agreed we'd keep in touch and shook hands, slapping one another on the back. *I'll miss this guy*, I thought. I hoped to see Jim again soon, despite the envy that crept unwillingly into my soul. I covered it up with a smile. "McDermott, in case we miss each other in the morning, I wish you well with your travels and study."

He grinned, winked, and then turned for the steps. He was soon off to pursue his future, leaving me to find mine.

After Jim had gone to bed, I told the archbishop that I needed to stop back in the church to pray a bit before going to my room, so he led me back to the sanctuary.

Sitting in the front pew and looking up at the life-size crucifix with the statues of Mary and Joseph on either side, I took a long, deep breath. *You need to surrender*, I told myself, kneeling to pray. *God help me to be willing to do Your will... whatever that may be.*

Feeling hopeful, I got up and left the church and headed to my guest room in the rectory. The bed sure beat the one on the ship. I fell into it, exhausted. *Tomorrow I will begin my hunt for a good position and boarding house. For now, I need to fall off to sleep...*

CHAPTER 8

I woke up at ten the following morning, later than I'd slept in years. I sniffed the tantalizing aroma of bacon. It smelled like home, and I felt happy despite myself.

After dressing and descending the stairs, I was greeted by the hospitable archbishop. He informed me that McDermott rose early and said to say goodbye. "He's been on the train for an hour already." The housekeeper served me a scrumptious breakfast of bacon, eggs, toast, and coffee. I almost hugged her. It was the best breakfast I'd had since I left Ireland six weeks ago. Now that I felt energized, I was ready to tackle my new purpose in life. *God help me find the right one. I trust in you.*

Walking the New York streets immediately made me

wish I was instead strolling down to my family barn. Oh, how my heart ached, missing Aiden and the others, but mostly my priesthood dream. I knew I needed to snap out of this negativity and be positive, but gosh was it hard!

As I walked on, I noticed a George Washington equestrian statue smack in the middle of the town. As I studied it for quite a while, it gave me courage and a better attitude. I later came upon a few 'Help Wanted' signs, but they were for dock workers and railroad assistants. Those jobs were not what I had in mind.

I had an aptitude for working with numbers because of helping Pa with his farm business. We had to keep accurate records of the food we sold and the buying and selling of livestock. I searched for several hours, but nothing of interest appeared. Getting tired of walking, I stopped at a pub and had some tea.

A young chap about my age named Louis came by my table and said hello. We began talking. He told me he was a native of New York and was astute in business affairs. He was also kind and interested in my endeavors, and he gave me some good leads and directions on how to find them. Boy, what a blessing he was! After a lengthy conversation, we bid each other goodbye, and I once again felt encouraged. The following day I checked the first suggestion on my list Louis had given me. It was a bank in the heart of Manhattan, an attractive building with lots of windows. Advertisements blanketed most of the glass with the bank's special offers. That interview did not take long since the manager told me I was too young. He wanted an older person with experience. Apparently, he didn't feel farm business counted. I crossed that one out.

I then tried Louis's second idea. It was for a construction company quite a long distance away. I needed to ride on the horse drawn trolley to get there. That lead went nowhere too. Their position was filled by the time I arrived.

The third suggestion was not far from St. Monica's Church. It was a manufacturing company that needed a bookkeeper for their shoe business. I waited in the office for only a short time before the store owner came out to interview me. He introduced himself as Mr. Murphy and his round face and broad smile offered a hopeful welcome. He even had an Irish brogue, a definite good sign. Upon hearing his accent, I immediately relaxed. He seemed impressed with my credentials. We then went on a tour of his company. Inhaling the appealing smell of leather, I was even more drawn to the place. *I could learn to like it here.*

I was dumbfounded, however, when viewing the numerous aisles of shoes. Mr. Murphy said he started his business five years earlier and it was growing well. He then told me that the previous bookkeeper, an elderly gentleman, had to resign because of medical reasons. We returned to his office where he offered me the job.

I thought, *the luck of the Irish*, and I gladly accepted. Mr. Murphy told me I would start the following day. We discussed details and shook hands. Before leaving, I inquired about boarding houses. My new boss informed me of a place a mile and a half away. Leaving the shoe company, I breathed deeply, feeling my body tension melt away, thanking God for this relief.

CHAPTER 9

I settled on a room in the DeSantis Boarding House the next day. I was surprised there was a vacancy because of so many immigrants searching for a place to stay. Getting situated didn't take long. Mrs. DeSantis put me on the third floor. The steps were squeaky, but my room was cozy and smelled like bleach. I was fortunate about that since Mr. Murphy said many living quarters in New York, at least those that were affordable, were rather dirty and unappealing.

After plopping across the bed and stretching out, I started thinking about how long it would take before I made enough money for both McDermott and me to get by. Hours later I woke with a jolt, forgetting where I was. Sitting up in this new temporary home, I sighed. The luminous sun shone through my window and warmed the room. Summer was ending. It wouldn't be long before the chilly autumn air surrounded the city.

I decided to write to Aiden. Sadly, I had to report to him my enormous disappointment with all the details. I completed a seven-page letter. My heart poured out on each page.

I went downstairs for supper after I finished, appreciating the fact that my rent included two daily meals. Mrs. DeSantis proved to be an excellent cook as well as apartment manager and landlord. She had definite expectations of us boarders though. She commanded perfect cleanliness and proper behavior, and she forbade alcohol. She told us that the doors got locked promptly at ten—anyone who came back after that would have to sleep outside on the doorstep. She reminded me of a military sergeant. However, after I got to know her, I realized she had a good heart.

After dinner, I took a stroll around the yard and ventured around the neighborhood to become acclimated to the area. At dusk, I returned to the house to play my fiddle. That drew some folks around me in the parlor. After an hour of unintentional entertaining, two middle-aged men requested fiddle lessons. I gladly agreed, thinking it would bring in a little extra money. One chap said he owned a fiddle but had no time to play until now. The other man said he would buy one in a few days. Content with my first day at this new lodging, I retired to my room. *Maybe I can pay my debt to McDermott sooner than expected, especially if more people request lessons.* I then set my pocket watch to wake up early enough to attend morning Mass before starting work.

I was glad that St. Monica's Church wasn't too far from my boarding house. It began to drizzle on my way there the next morning, so I decided to shop for some more clothes, including a raincoat after work.

I wasted no time walking to the Murphy Shoe Company. My parents taught me that promptness was important, and I certainly wanted to make a good impression. Upon entering, one of the factory workers greeted me. He was a congenial chap and made conversation. In the middle of our discussion, Mr. Murphy appeared pleased and shook my hand.

"You are good and prompt, Joe. I like that in my employees. Excuse me, fellows, for interrupting, but I need to escort Joe to his new office." We went around a corner and down a long hallway, then turned and went down a second hallway. My office was at the end of that hall. The desk was flooded with papers and ledgers. What a sight!

"Our previous man didn't have time to clean up before he had to leave. Don't let this mess discourage you, Joe. I have faith you can handle it after a few days of orienting yourself and getting organized. I will be in to give you information when needed, and you can call on Mr. Smith, our assistant bookkeeper, with any additional questions. He has been with us for three years and knows the ropes. His office is the one behind yours."

"Yes, sir. I will certainly do my best with tackling all of this, and I am happy to be here." *Where to begin?* I wondered.

"Oh, and Joe, noon is break time."

"Aye."

Purchase receipts, sales receipts, payment transactions, and financial statements all covered my desk from one end to the other. Every inch of wood was blanketed. *Well, this is nothing like Pa's neat little office space at home.* I needed to begin putting papers in piles and categories, one at a time, checking each one individually. I got down to work and before long I had three piles of papers grouped in different categories. I just had to continue this until I was organized. I realized it would take days.

At lunch, I met Mr. Smith. He told me to call him William. He was about six years older than me and rather quiet. From our conversation, I could tell he was a real asset to this company. Although he was a modest man, he informed me of some valuable knowledge regarding the system of Murphy's business expenses.

"Why didn't you request this position of bookkeeper?"

I asked him.

"I enjoy traveling to Baltimore rather frequently to visit my family. Being in charge here would limit my possibilities."

"I see." I felt lucky to have this kind man helping me, realizing it would be a tough job to fill. I knew from working with Pa that it was imperative to stay current on inventory. Otherwise, you could find yourself in a deep financial mess. My father instilled in me that bookkeeping was a time-consuming task and I needed to be accurate. "Meticulous" is a word I recalled him using.

The rest of the day seemed to fly by. On the way back to the boarding house, I had to shop for a few pieces of clothing. William mentioned a store down by the railroad station. Being short of money, I needed to only purchase necessities. Later, after working for several weeks, I could add a few more pieces once I began paying McDermott his fee.

The second day was a repeat of the first. When Mr. Murphy greeted me, he told me after working for six months I would be entitled to a free pair of shoes. This was a bonus for all his workers, no matter which department they served. He added it would then be considered an annual bonus. After four days, I had enough piles of paper to fill all of Pa's milk cans. I began feeling organized.

"Joe, I am impressed with your ability to handle this monumental job. You have certainly proven yourself within such a short time," Mr. Murphy told me at the end of the day.

"Thank you, sir."

"Tomorrow we can start tackling all our current financial transactions. I am pleased with your work, son."

Strolling back to my place, I whispered a little prayer of thanks and began humming the tune, "When Irish Eyes Are Smiling."

The Coin Flip

CHAPTER 10

Weeks rolled into months. The dreary, damp, drizzly fall season of New York seemed worse than Ireland's weather. Spotting red berry shrubs sitting among the bare deciduous tree branches gave me hope for better days. At least my work room was a warm refuge.

With large orders being requested almost daily, it was obvious our shoe business was growing nicely. New shoe designs were being created regularly by a few staff members. The different styles were appealing even to people like me who didn't give a hoot about style. Many customers would visit our company for individual purchases, although most shoes and boots were sent out in large quantities to small local shops and shipped out of state to other big cities, like Boston and Chicago.

One day, when William and I had some extra time at work to talk, I invited him into my little office. We pulled back our chairs and he crossed his legs while I rested my feet on top of my desk. “If I smoked, I’d offer you a cigarette, but it’s not for me,” I said.

“My grandpa favors cigars which I find nauseating, so smoking turns me off, too.”

“Does he live with you?”

“No. He lives with my parents and sister in Baltimore. Both he and my grandma do. They help my mother with my sister since she suffers with tuberculosis. The doctor said we are lucky it hasn’t developed into active tuberculosis bacteria. That can be fatal.”

“Oh William, I am so sorry! What a trial.”

“Well, she’s usually in good spirits, so that’s a blessing.

She's smart too, has a contract with the local newspaper writing a weekly column about classical composers and their music. Mother delivers them for her each week."

"No kidding. That's interesting. Does your family prefer classical music?"

"Not me. I do like it sometimes, especially Vivaldi, but I prefer a nice variety, even opera occasionally. How about you, Joe?"

"Oh, my favorite is Irish, but folk music is my second favorite. One weekend when you're not busy, let's go out and unwind by listening to some music. There are many taverns around here."

"Yeah, let's. Also, I have a checkerboard if you're up to losing a few games," William said with a grin.

"Sure. How long have you been playing?"

"Since I was a young lad. My father taught me since it has always been his favorite pastime. Yet, he had no remorse when he would always beat me. He never let me win. Therefore, I was determined to learn strategies to beat him. Finally, it happened when I was thirteen years old. He was flabbergasted. Since then, we take turns winning."

"I see. Maybe you should join tournaments?"

"Heck no. I enjoy playing just for fun. We better get back to work now. We don't want to take advantage of Mr. Murphy's easy-going manner."

"Absolutely not."

In November, I was elated to receive a lengthy letter from Aiden. My heart swelled as I read his words.

"Dear Joe,

I was thrilled to receive your letter, but also shocked and most sad to hear of your coin toss and extreme disappointment. You are a mighty strong person, Joe, to accept the outcome so graciously. I told the family what you said, and Ma and Pa couldn't believe their ears. We are all sorry for what happened. Maybe though, in the long run, it will work out best for you. Everything happens for a reason.

In spite of that, we are glad you landed a job to your liking and found a good place to live. As time goes on, write about American life. We are anxious to hear how things are there.

Now, about life here... One of the goats ate a hole right through Pa's overalls the other night. That really surprised him. Your favorite pig, Elsie, finally had her babe. Pa decided to name it Eoj (your name spelled backwards - ha, ha). The apple trees grew well this year. The crop was plentiful enough that we were able to sell about fifteen bushels. The Conlon's built a pier for their pond. It was the biggest draw this summer. We were over there as often as possible. One day, Sam came out of the water and realized two crappies were flipping around inside his drawers. That was funny! You should have seen him dancin' round.

We have new neighbors over the hill. They own a one-

hundred-pound golden retriever. He is a fun, frisky dog. He comes over to visit with their boy, who is Pat's age. The boys sometimes use the dog as a pillow. Other times, I see them running with him through the hay loft.

Ma's quilt was voted the prettiest one in her sewing circle. She's giving it to Aunt Sharon for Christmas.

I have some parish news, too. Father Dorn is celebrating his fortieth anniversary next month, so the sodality is planning a big reception for him in the parish hall. It's supposed to be a surprise, but we think he has guessed.

Well, bye for now, Joe. Stay well. Enjoy your new endeavors.

Your best friend and brother, Aiden."

The letter brought joy, but also a feeling of homesickness. It rejuvenated my spirit and gave me hope, but at the same time, I started questioning my intention. Was I doing the right thing working here, or should I return to Ireland and send money to McDermott from there now that I no longer was going to enter the seminary and study to be a priest? My mind was puzzled. Trying to ignore my feelings, I simply repressed them.

When Christmas Eve arrived, I stopped by William's office at the end of the day and gave him a figure of a small vessel I had carved, wrapped in newspaper and tied with cord.

"I was completely unaware of this talent of yours, Joe. I appreciate this lovely gift."

"Oh sure. It's relaxing to do. You might want to try it some time."

"Tomorrow, I'm taking the ferry to Baltimore to visit my folks. Do you care to join me?"

"Well, thanks anyways, but I think I will stay put. I have two fiddle lessons I'm giving this week, and some reading to do."

"How are the lessons coming along?"

"One man is doing very well. He plans to join his

friends when they play for jigs. The other one is struggling. He said he might soon change to some other instrument. Well, William, I wish you a jolly Christmas and blessings always."

"You have a good holiday too, Joe."

"Aye."

CHAPTER 11

Christmas morning Mass at St. Monica's was beautiful. White poinsettias alternated with red roses semi-circled the altar and cascaded down the middle of the steps. Bright gold stars hung between all of the wooden Stations of the Cross, and one huge white star made of satin hung above the altar. A garland of pinecones and greens outlined the windows. On each window shelf sat a plain, twelve-inch fir tree. The eight-foot Christmas tree stood in the left corner of the altar. Twinkling blue lights flooded the tree from top to bottom, enhancing the blue porcelain nativity scene underneath.

Some children performed a little skit before Mass began. They reenacted the nativity with costumes their mothers made. One little boy, who played a Wise man, forgot his line and began crying from embarrassment. The little girl beside him whispered to him what to say. Another child, portraying an angel, lifted his robe to scratch his leg. The boy next to him nudged him to stop and the child yelled out, "I have an itch!" The audience could not hold their laughter. The two live lambs had thick green bows tied around their necks. One lamb decided to voice his greeting which made the children giggle. Since I sat up front, the smell of the straw caused me to feel momentarily nostalgic. Candles supplied the only light until Mass began. I felt locked in this scene, still and peaceful.

The choir, consisting of both men and women dressed in their red robes, sang six Christmas carols with the help of a pianist, flute player, and trumpet player. The congregation was directed to join in when singing "Silent Night." The fragrance of incense coupled with singing caused me to feel a spiritual high. I thanked Archbishop Kearney for a memorable Christmas Mass as he passed out candy canes to the children as they left. The church bells rang "Joy to the World" as we all went on our way.

After it was over, McDermott spied me as all the people filed out and suggested we visit over coffee. I was glad to see him, and happily agreed. We went to the famous pub a block away from church called Aaron's. It was decorated in a most festive style for the holidays. A wreath on the door added some humor since it was made of beer mugs. The owner included a drink on the house for the first round to celebrate Christmas. We cheered each other with, "Slante!" Being anxious and curious to hear about his studies, I dove right in and asked, "How are your classes coming along McDermott?"

"Well, I can't lie, they are terribly harder than I expected. Lots of work and not much time for leisure. I like my professors, though. One especially is so personable. He tells us stories of his family and life experiences all the time. He's downright entertaining. But I have to say, I'm pleased that I could return here to St. Monica's for a two-week breather. The archbishop said I can help him with his duties in exchange for room and board." He yawned, then apologized and said,

"What about your work?"

"I like it. My boss is a fine man, and my coworkers are kind. I enjoy what I do. We're always busy. I'm learning it's a most progressive company, and I don't have any homework." I said that last remark with tongue in cheek.

"Happy to hear that, Quigley."

"Have you heard from your family recently, McDermott?" I asked.

"I received one letter in October and another one just last week. Have you?"

"Yeah, mine came in November from my brother. I sure wish the mail could be delivered faster. It's so good to hear news from back home."

"I'll say. I hope you know how thankful I am for the money you send me each week, Quigley. That goes for my parents, too. You are a fine and noble gentleman. Your character is exemplary."

"You would be doing the same if it were reversed."

"I'm glad we can keep in touch."

"Aye. Well, this coffee was enough to warm us for our walk. Good seeing you, McDermott. Enjoy your holiday and study hard."

"Merry Christmas to you, Quigley."

Walking home, I reflected on our visit, recalling my quiet voice, and chiding myself for having to clear my throat too many times. Hoping my inner confusion and jealousy were not noticeable to McDermott, I took a long, deep breath and raised my head to the exhilarating scent of chimney smoke. It has always been one of my favorite smells. I remembered as a kid, I would frequently sit outside on our porch on a cold and still winter night to simply sniff the chimney smoke of nearby houses. Gazing at the stars added to the delight. Ma told me I had the biggest sniffer in all of Ireland.

It took time for me to fall asleep that night as I recalled all the magnificent splendor of the Christmas Mass. Winter was harsh. Many days, I could barely see beyond two feet in front of me when walking to work. The snow and wind were blinding at times. Twice I fell on the ice. Once it caused a sprained ankle, but the other time I caught myself. Mrs. DeSantis apologized a few times for only fixing soup rather than a full-course dinner because it was too difficult to get out to the store. No one complained. Her soups were delicious.

Still, I missed life on our family farm, spending hours with my siblings and all the neighbors sled riding, having snowball battles and ice skating on the overflow from the spring house, then coming home to warm up with Ma's hot chocolate and heated apple cake.

My childhood memories seemed distant now, relegated to a long-ago time and place. Now experiencing adulthood, I can understand why parents would say, "Enjoy your childhood, because time goes so fast."

CHAPTER 12

Little by little, I began falling into a state of depression. I noticed it happening about a year or so after I began at the shoe company. It wasn't my job because I liked what I did. I think my disappointment over my fate and the loss of my priesthood dream were still taking a toll. My friend, William, observed the extent of it one afternoon at work.

"Joe, you've seemed downtrodden for too long. I was hoping it was just going to be a short period of time before you snapped out of it. But that was several weeks ago. I believe you need to seek professional help."

"As much as I appreciate my work, I still wish I could be in the seminary. I've been trying to accept God's will, but the agony has surfaced."

"Why don't you talk to Archbishop Kearney? You said you like him and perhaps he could help you through this?"

"Thanks, William. Perhaps I might."

The following morning, I spoke to the archbishop after Mass. I asked him if I could make an appointment to talk with him sometime soon when he had a chance.

"Of course, Joe. I have time in the evening next week. Which day would you like?"

"Any day except Tuesday. That's when I give a fiddle lesson."

"Ok. Let's meet here Monday at seven."

"Thank you, Archbishop. I appreciate your time. See you then."

When Monday evening arrived, I knocked on the rectory door. The archbishop beckoned me into his modest but attractive office. I stared at the gallery of pictures he'd hung on the largest wall. “You like them, Joe? My buddy sent them after his travels to all those different parks. He was always into exploring. He sat at his big oak desk. “Happy to see you. Now, sit down over there on the sofa. Can I get you something to drink?”

“No thank you, sir.”

“Well then, how can I help you?”

“As you know Archbishop, I have felt terribly disappointed about losing the coin toss. I thought I would get over it and feel better soon. However, it’s been over a year now, and I am starting to feel worse. I know everything happens for a reason, and I’m trying to accept God’s will, but it’s tough.”

“Disappointments happen in all of our lives, Joe, some more than others. And yes, they can be heavy crosses. When we pray for the grace of acceptance, and trust in Jesus, things do work out. I suggest going on the annual one week retreat that St. Joseph’s offers this spring. It will start the first week of May and is only about twenty miles from here. I have been summoned to help out with Masses and a talk, so you may ride with me if you like."

"Hmmm, maybe so. I would need to request an early vacation week if my boss would allow that. I guess it's worth a try. I've never been on a retreat before."

"I believe you will find it most helpful."

"Is it expensive? I don't have much money left over after saving each week what I need to send to McDermott."

"Don't worry, son. It goes by donation only. Besides, Fr. Cronin always teases in his Irish humor saying that anyone who has trouble paying can do his laundry for a month and teach his horse to talk. That seems to put everyone at ease."

"I guess it would," I replied with a smirk. "Is there anything special I need to bring?"

"Only whatever you need for a week's stay. Relax now. You will meet some good people and should enjoy it all to the fullest."

"Alright, Archbishop. I appreciate what you said. Thanks."

After leaving the rectory, I took a long walk. March was here and the freezing temperatures had finally subsided a bit, and walking had become a little easier. The bright streetlights encouraged me to go further than I anticipated. My thoughts of what the archbishop said were interrupted when I heard a little cry in a distance. My curiosity carried me around the corner. Creeping closer, I saw a cat trying to fight off a wandering dog. Looking around, I grabbed a tree limb and frightened the intruder away. After licking itself, the cat looked up at me as if to say, 'thank you,' then trailed off.

That incident somehow reminded me of St. Francis. The fresh night air swept through my veins allowing me to breathe deeply and continue walking for a while longer. The neighborhood was conducive for walking because of the flat pebbled paths. It was a tranquilizing stroll, especially when the owls and thrush kept me company.

The next morning, I was relieved to hear what Mr. Murphy said when I consulted him about taking time off.

"Well, son, I have a cousin who benefitted from yearly retreats. He kept trying to encourage the whole family to attend. He didn't get anywhere with stubborn me, but I certainly don't deny others their chance. Go and enjoy when the time comes. You will still have another week to use later in the year."

"Thanks, Mr. Murphy. I'll make sure the books are current when I leave." I finally felt a glimmer of hope amidst the depression and doubt. *Well Lord, hopefully this retreat will help,* I prayed repeatedly for a few minutes. I was also thinking of how lucky I was to have such an understanding and kind boss.

CHAPTER 13

The archbishop met me at the horse-drawn street trolley check-in. Two beautiful, shiny black draft horses stamped their hooves, ready to lead.

The conductor collected our tickets and showed us to our seats. We chatted for a while. Then the archbishop dozed off while I took in the scenery. Since St. Joseph's parish was only twenty miles away, I was able to enjoy the ride without becoming weary of too long a distance. The May flowers were in bloom and the newborn leaves burst with their lime-colored hues. A soft brushing of clouds flowed across the sky. It was indeed a good day for a ride.

It took us about five hours to reach St. Joseph's parish,

which was northwest of Manhattan. The church was quaint, built of hewn granite stone, with a steeple and red painted wooden doors. It reminded me of one in Mayo. Inside, the yellow walls and ceilings were like sunshine, illuminating our souls. I figured it certainly was the perfect setting for a retreat.

We met Father Cronin, the pastor. He was shorter than average, with twinkling eyes and an opened-mouth smile which exposed one gold tooth. His jovial demeanor immediately put me at ease. There was a total of thirty other male retreatants ranging in age from their late teens to fifty years old. I heard some say they came from as far away as New Jersey and Delaware. One gentleman told me it was his fourth year attending.

After our meet and greet, we were served a hearty supper in the dining hall, which held two long rectangular tables. We all complimented the chef, Father Ford, for his excellent choice of roast pork, mashed potatoes, green beans, and a variety of fresh cut fruit topped with homemade cream. When dinner was over, we were given an itinerary for the week and then retired to our rooms. My room was meticulously clean and looked just like what I would expect a monk's room to resemble, replete with a bed, desk, chair, bureau, and crucifix.

The next day we had Mass and listened to a reflection during breakfast and then were given time for private prayer. Father Cronin told us to feel free to wander around the grounds. The spring flowers brightened the jade carpet surrounding the outside of the church. The lawn reminded me of our shamrock-covered fields back home, and I felt my heart lift. The foliage and the colorful hawthorns evoked memories of Ma's garden border. I breathed it all in, the smells of fresh-cut grass and white honeysuckles, remembering the story my mother told me about when she was little and made a necklace out of honeysuckles for her mother. My heart ached with bittersweet memories, but at the same time I was comforted by my surroundings.

Confession was offered. I took advantage of admitting sorrow for not fully trusting Jesus in my current state, and of course my other sins of anger, jealousy and impatience. I felt the healing of repentance and was reminded of God's everlasting love, mercy and forgiveness. Adoration was held. Being able to worship our Lord who was truly present in the appearance of a white wafer was extremely comforting.

The retreat wasn't considered private, but I noticed most of the participants preferred being to themselves, praying or reading.

I wandered off in the afternoon to the library, which was full of enticing books and pamphlets. I came across an old copy of *The Dark Night of the Soul* by St. John of the Cross. The edges were slightly frayed which indicated its popularity. I was instinctively drawn to the brownish-colored pages as if it was written just for me. Becoming instantly lost in this gem, it seemed word after word was implanted in my spirit. The spiritual emptiness and transformation of St. John was parallel to my own spiritual life. I could not have read anything more helpful. I was so engrossed in my reading I didn't hear the dinner bell ring, and someone had to personally call me to supper that night.

When we finished supper that evening, Archbishop Kearney gave an excellent talk on the deep, eternal love that God has for His people. A large part of his sermon included how Jesus suffers along with us in all our pain and trials, and that we are not alone. "God has a plan for us and leads us forward," the archbishop said. "He will never abandon us but instead He will walk with us. There is merit in suffering, and every person has worth and value. Every soul is treasured. We need to try to offer up our pain along with the pain Christ suffered on Calvary. When we try to follow His plan, we can be assured of it succeeding and enriching our soul. God's wellspring of peace will flood us when we surrender and trust in Him.

I never heard a more profound message. It sure made me think hard about my situation. I knew in that moment I needed to kill my self-pity and walk on before it killed me. *Only by your grace, Lord.*

The rest of the week followed in a similar way. Each day I could feel the Holy Spirit pouring Its grace upon my heart. It was an experience I will never forget.

Riding home, the archbishop and I both said the Rosary and read some of the books we purchased from the sale table. I thanked him for recommending this memorable experience.

"Yes, it was indeed enlightening and well-organized. And remember, son, with all that was said, humility has a big part in all of it."

Humility. I sure need to beg for that virtue. Perhaps that is my trouble, I am too proud.

Back at work, William said I looked like a new person, and he was happy for me that I went, but was also glad to have me back. "The statements and invoices were yelling for you. Even though I do fine, I don't have your knack for managing this office."

"William, don't underestimate yourself, buddy. You're a key operator here."

In June, William surprised me with an invitation to my

first professional baseball game. The Yankees were going to play against the Brooklyn Atlantics. His neighbor was able to buy tickets if we could go.

"I have never been to a professional game. Sounds fun!"

"Good. Then I'll tell my neighbor to include us. The game is on July twentieth. He needs to purchase tickets ahead of time to secure them."

"Thanks, I can't wait, especially since I have never even played baseball. This will be a new experience. You need to explain the rules to me, William."

"Of course. It's easy. You'll like it. I played often when I was a kid. I remember one day, when I was about ten years old, I played with a few friends. I pitched the ball to the batter and accidentally hit his head. He collapsed and it looked like I knocked him out cold. I was terrified, thinking I either killed him or injured him badly. We all ran over to him and hovered with worry. I panicked and said, 'Oh Jack, I'm so sorry, can you hear me?' He jumped up and said, 'Gotcha,' and laughed. We were all relieved, but I felt like punching him. That guy always was a jokester."

"That's funny," Quigley said.

"Now it is, but back then it wasn't."

The night of the game was full of fun. Fans cheered wildly at every crack of the bat. I never heard so much excitement at one time. What a game! Even though soccer has always been and is my favorite sport, I now admit baseball is a close second. We treated ourselves to hotdogs, peanuts, and sodas, and had a grand time.

That night I wrote a letter to Aiden. I needed to tell him about the retreat and the ball game. I mentioned, too, that I was finally getting used to city living even though I still preferred the country, but at least I was having some fun and finally feeling less homesick.

Autumn was busier than ever at work. More and more shoe sales kept coming our way. The new styles our company devised became popular across the East Coast. Mr. Murphy told me that he might need to hire another bookkeeper at the beginning of the year. I thought it wouldn't be a bad idea since papers were piling up all over the place.

He began attending more meetings with bankers. One week he needed to travel to Boston to discuss his shoe business with several merchants. He came back home with the idea of expanding his factory up north.

In February, a new chap named Henry was added to work with William and me. Henry caught on fast and was immediately an asset to the company. By the following winter, another man, named Lawrence, was hired.

It was soon after that, I thought about opening my own store.

The Coin Flip

CHAPTER 14

Working with Murphy Shoe Company for three years was a fruitful experience. It made me feel confident about beginning my own business. I wanted to sell shoes since I knew so much about that business, but I also wanted to provide plenty of other merchandise. Owning a general store to accommodate more of what the public needed seemed logical. I wanted it to be in Pittsburgh, Pennsylvania since I had some older relatives who had settled there prior to the famine. I wrote to Pa, and he wrote back with their address in case I would ever want to contact them.

Timing was important. I didn't want to leave Mr. Murphy in a pinch and did not care to move to Pittsburgh in the challenging winter months. I decided on the late summer as my appointed time, which would give Mr. Murphy a few months to find a replacement.

"I'm happy for you, Joe, but I'm sorry you won't be staying with us," he said sadly when I told him my decision.

"Well, Mr. Murphy, you can be sure I won't leave until your replacement arrives."

I, too, was sorry to leave the friendships I had made, especially the one I had with William, although we promised to keep in touch.

I went over to church to say goodbye to Archbishop Kearney. Since McDermott was still attending summer classes, I couldn't see him, so I wrote a note to him at Christ the King seminary, informing him of my plan.

I told McDermott to come visit me after I relocated. "I'll send you my address when I'm settled, and will look forward to seeing you when you're able," I wrote.

After writing to him, another wave of disappointment crept over me about missing the priesthood. This feeling still haunted me occasionally. I learned that trying to deal with it was better than ignoring it. The retreat had helped. I kept re-playing the thought that my craving and passion for becoming a priest wasn't what God wanted, it was only my desire. *His will is what counts in life*, I reminded myself. Wrestling with this was painful, but I knew trusting Him was my healing.

When the time came for my departure, I had already paid McDermott a quarter of my debt. I was able to increase the sum to half when I received a surprise gift from Mr. Murphy who gave me a generous present on my last day with him. "Joe, you have been an outstanding worker and I appreciate all your help." My employer handed me an envelope filled with a wad of bills. "I have considered you a son. Your parents must be so proud of you. Please keep in touch and let me know how your new business works out. Let me know if I can ever assist you in any way."

I looked down in amazement at the cash in my hands,

holding back tears. "I am more than grateful to you, sir. Working here has been a blessing. Yes, I would like to keep in touch. Thank you for everything."

The next day I boarded the train to Pittsburgh, PA. The locomotive's interior was impressive to say the least. The red velvet seats were a surprise. They felt more comfortable than some beds. The shiny, wood paneling was attractive with some paintings interspersed. There was plenty of illumination from fancy fixtures. Even the windows were notable with their heavy, brocade patterned drapes. I didn't expect it to be so fancy and accommodating. Since it was my first time traveling on the rails, I sat back and enjoyed the ride, and even visited the dining car to sample their cuisine.

In there, I met some distinguished gentlemen who had been to Pittsburgh and were returning on business. They spoke at length to me about the town since I mentioned that I hadn't been there yet. The one man with a black mustache vocalized his pleasure of the place. "Pittsburgh has lots of industry and plenty of industrial work, especially in iron, glass, petroleum, and farm goods. The economy is booming." That sounded good to me. He added, "I find the people are a friendly bunch, and the three rivers, the Ohio, Monongahela, and Allegheny, and numerous hills make for ravish scenery. You will like living there." My heart delighted with excitement of learning more about my new home. My uncertainty melted away the more they talked.

"I'm looking forward to it, sir," I replied with a smile. "I have a few distant relatives there, so hopefully we can connect soon after my arrival."

The taller man with a white beard asked, "What sort of business are you involved with?"

"I'm a bookkeeper, and after I acquire a position there, I then plan to open my own general store."

"Good idea. They could surely use one from what I found."

After our extended meal and visit, we headed back to our assigned cars. Leaning back on my seat, I fell asleep, thanking God for what these strangers told me. It gave me added encouragement.

The following day we arrived at our destination. With my insides yelling *hurrah*, and with energy about to break through my skin, I departed the train. My impatience surfaced, but this time in a good way and for good reason.

With suitcase in hand and pulling my trunk, I asked the train conductor to direct me to the nearest boarding house. When he told me how far from the station it was, I decided to hire a carriage. In the six- or seven-mile ride we passed a factory with a "Help Wanted" sign in the front window. It was a textile mill. I wrote down the name and address and planned to visit the next day.

In the boarding house, three men were playing cards in the parlor. They invited me to join, saying they preferred playing with partners. One introduced himself as Tim McGovern, one was Damien O'Neill, and the third was Roy Hahn. I did enjoy playing Whist before going to my assigned room. We played a good while and fell into conversation.

“You’re apparently new in town,” one man said as he gathered up the cards.

“Aye, just arrived actually. I have relatives who live somewhere in this town and would like to look them up.”

“What’re their names?”

“The Quigleys.”

“Hmmm, it wouldn’t be Thomas J. Quigley by any chance?”

“Why yes indeed! Do you know him?”

“I met a chap by that name a year ago at a church social. He lives outside of town past the steel mill. He is a friendly character and rather funny, too, if I may say so.”

“Glad to know. Thanks Mr. McGovern.”

“Call me Tim. Will you be staying here for long?”

“Yes, I’m looking for work, so I’ll be here indefinitely.”

"Check out the newspaper over there on the table, plenty of ads in there," Mr. O'Neill chimed in.

"Okay. Will do. Where do you fellows work?"

"Damien and Tim work on the railroad," answered Roy, "and I work in the coal mine. Both have been prospering in the last several years."

When we said goodnight, I took the newspaper up to my room.

CHAPTER 15

After a good night's sleep, I eagerly paged through the paper to find the employment ads. I spotted a few requesting help with bookkeeping. There were two textile mill offers. One was the same as the sign I saw in the shopfront yesterday. There were three others from petroleum plants.

I spent the next several days investigating and interviewing for them all. They all sounded appealing. With lots of discernment, I chose a textile company since I had previous experience with shoes. Shoes are not clothes or fabric, but I figured the two were more similar than petroleum. My boss, Mr. Dennis, asked me to begin as soon as possible. I was glad the job hunt was over.

That evening, sitting in the white wicker rocker on our large front porch, Roy Hahn came over and started talking. The fragrant autumn trees with their leaves of vibrant colors surrounded us and made me feel relaxed.

Roy informed me of the local churches, stores, taverns, and people in our vicinity, which was a big help. He volunteered information about his limp, which he said was work-related. We had a long chat as the sun set. Feeling chilly and sleepy, we slowly rose, stretched, and retired to our rooms.

The next day I set out to find the church, Queen of Peace, of which Roy spoke. It was beautifully constructed with ornate décor, and was relatively new, unlike St. Monica's in New York. They held daily morning Mass, which was convenient for workers. I was impressed with the hand-carved statue of the Holy Family made by an elderly parishioner. The life-size sculpture of the Pieta was stunning. The word "Sanctus" was engraved three times across the base of the altar, and there was a statue of Mary standing outside by the front door with one arm outstretched, welcoming people.

Touring around town, I stumbled upon a shoe store. Browsing up and down the aisles, I read some of the labels and realized they were manufactured in Murphy's shoe factory. *Wow, what'll you know, I'll be darned.*

Leaving there, I ventured into an Irish pub. Almost feeling at home, I ordered Shepherd's Pie. That brought on a feeling of nostalgia along with a sign hanging on the wall near my seat that advertised a weekly jig held in town. I recalled the weekly entertainment back home in Mickey's tavern, a favorite hangout since Mickey's opened earlier and closed later than the other pubs.

On my walk home, I bought some books at the corner bookstore. A feeling of contentment flooded through me as I whistled unhurriedly all the way back home. I started to think I would like it here in Pittsburgh, much more than New York City.

It encouraged me to write to Aiden that evening and tell him all about my new home.

At the textile factory, there were more workers than at Murphy's shoe company. The routine for us bookkeepers was similar though. I quickly understood the work assigned to me, and dove right in. Since I could grasp my duties with no trouble, I offered to work overtime when needed. I wanted to make the extra money since the balance of my debt to McDermott was hanging over my head. I hoped it wouldn't be more than a couple of years before it was completely paid.

Week after week, I fell into a regular routine. That presented the opportunity of visiting the pub on Saturday nights to hear the music. I persuaded my card friends to come when they could.

After frequenting the place, the owner noticed that I was a weekly patron. He came over one night to talk with me. He was a friendly chap. I expressed my appreciation of all the music played in his place, especially the Irish songs. Then he asked, "Do you play an instrument?"

"Yes, I play the fiddle."

"Then how about joining in with my players? We can always use another fella. The more the merrier, I always say."

I was overjoyed and immediately accepted. That added a social dimension to my life. No money was given, but I received plenty of free food and drink. That didn't even matter though, it was just fun.

I sent my Pittsburgh relatives a Christmas card and mentioned my new address. In January, a generous dinner invitation arrived. *Oh good, now I will be able to meet some of the family members. It's been four years since I've been home. Seeing some distant family should ease the ache.* I planned my visit for the end of the month.

In no time I was on my way to Uncle Tom and Aunt Kate's. They could not have been more hospitable. After about a dozen hugs and handshakes were shared, we sat down in their modest but clean parlor to begin our long-awaited reunion. I noticed Uncle Tom resembled Pa, or I should say Pa resembled him with the dark brown hair and his tall slim stature. The only difference was he didn't have the same cheek dimple. Aunt Kate needed to use a cane, although it didn't detract from her smiling Irish eyes, milky complexion, and short, graying curls.

"Aunt Kate, you look way younger than I pictured."

"Oh Joe, that's malarkey, but thanks anyways, dear."

A few minutes later, their sons, Michael and Owen, came in from their nearby homes with their families and the hugs started all over again. Liam, their youngest son and my uncle, only six years my senior, greeted us an hour or so later when he finished working in the fields. His five o'clock shadow on his long face showed below his wavy, chestnut hair. Their daughter Katie was married and lived in the Midwest. A picture of her sat on top of the old square grand piano alongside other cherished photos.

In total, there were sixteen of us gathered together. A party suddenly erupted. Tea and scones were immediately devoured. Aunt Kate and the two wives disappeared in the kitchen while all my cousins, ages five through sixteen, played and laughed and asked me questions faster than I could answer.

"Whoa," Owen said to the younger kids. "Let Joe rest a bit and answer one at a time."

"Oh, it's ok," I replied with a grin. It's grand to see family again."

Amidst all of the commotion, my cousins Nora and Molly filled the table by Aunt Kate's direction with an array of food—dishes of sausage, stuffing, potatoes, parsnips, roast beef, kale, and so much more. It could have fed an army. My uncle said a blessing and made our famous family toast. "Here's to us, better people there ain't."

When the scrumptious meal was completed by all, music and singing was provided by those who wanted to display their talents. Two cousins said they sang in the church choir and began harmonizing, while two others and myself accompanied them with our instruments— me on my fiddle, and two others on a flute and a guitar. I was glad I decided to bring my fiddle with me in hopes that this might occur.

I glanced over at Aunt Kate and noticed tears of joy in her sparkling blue-green eyes as she sat with her hands folded in her lap, smiling like an angel, reminding me of Ma.

The frolicking continued until the young clan started falling asleep in corners. The adult conversation cascaded into the midnight hour. It was a night to remember, and I couldn't wait to rehash it all in a letter to my folks back home in Ireland.

CHAPTER 16

Katie's old bedroom was converted into a guest room for me. Her antique bed was warm and cozy. I woke feeling grateful for a long, sound sleep. We dressed for a late Mass, and then came home to enjoy a true Irish breakfast of fried eggs, tomatoes, potatoes, sausage, white pudding, bread, and tea and orange juice.

Liam invited me to go with him for a walk around the barn and field. We dressed in layers since the temperature was only a few degrees above freezing. It felt invigorating to be in the open field.

He showed me their two new sheep and a baby lamb. Their barn contained a trap door for the purpose of dropping hay for the cows. Of course, the cousins used it for playing hide-and-seek and as a quick getaway when chasing each other. Liam admitted he even joined in the fun when they were visiting. After stretching our legs, we headed back to the cottage. I asked him why he wasn't married. "Oh, just haven't found the right girl, but maybe someday."

"Well, I suppose I best be saying my goodbyes to all you lovely folks," I said later that morning, wishing I could stay longer but realizing I had to get back to work the next day. "As much as I hate to leave, I need to get back home before dark. I truly appreciate your hospitality Aunt Kate and Uncle Tom. Thank you for having me. It meant so much. Liam, so good to see you. Let me know when you shear those sheep, maybe I can come and help," I cheerfully offered, and meant every word. *It would do my heart good to do some farm work again.*

"We are happy you could be here. Please come again," said Uncle Tom. Aunt Kate tucked a little package in my coat pocket as she kissed me goodbye.

The train ride back to my boarding house seemed to go quickly since I was completely immersed in daydreaming about the past twenty-four hours. Noticing the Irish bread in the parcel from my aunt, I decided to save it for work the next day. When I returned home and ascended the steps to my room, I thanked God for the amusing weekend and family fun, but also for the gift of work.

The next day at the office was as usual except for one thing... my co-worker, Paul, forgot to put in his dentures before coming to work. When he spoke, his mouth looked drawn together like a tiny baby's. I had to swallow my laugh and lock my lips together to keep from causing a scene. The poor man admitted feeling embarrassed, but he said it was too far a distance to return home for them. "I will just have to swallow my pride whenever I talk to anyone today," he confided in me.

"Oh, don't worry, you'll make their day," I replied with a wink and a pat on his shoulder. He chuckled and shook his head. It felt good to laugh.

In early spring, I received a letter from McDermott. He told me he was coming to Pittsburgh and asked if I would like to visit when he was in town at Queen of Peace to help during Holy Week. "Sure," I wrote back. "It will be good to see you, McDermott." Three weeks later, I met him in the rectory after work. We had supper at a famous oyster house. Neither of us had ever eaten oysters before. "I keep hearing people rave about these culinary delights," I said, excited to try something new.

"Ok with me. I've heard that they're delicious, so this is a good chance as any to find out."

"Mr. Dennis, my boss, said there are different ways to eat them. We can slurp raw ones or have them fried or in a stew."

"I think I'll choose the stew. Slurping needs to be demonstrated first."

"I'll go with that, too."

After placing our order, we relaxed with a beer and

began chatting.

"This is my first visit to Pennsylvania," McDermott said.

"Well, I like it here and the folks are friendly. It isn't as congested as New York City. I was drawn here because of some relatives who I met up with recently."

"Quigley, even though I miss the Emerald Isle, I do enjoy living here in America. I heard from one of my brothers who has decided he wants to move here in a few years when he is a bit older. He told me that New York sounded appealing." My friend looked at me, questioning concern in his blue eyes. He paused a moment and then asked hesitantly, "How are things with you?"

"I'm good. I know everything will work out. I'll have you know that I am learning to be more patient. Isn't that a miracle?" I said, trying to be witty.

We reminisced about our voyage to America and compared St. Monica's to Queen of Peace while enjoying our oyster stew.

"I have to say, this truly was a satisfying meal." McDermott folded his napkin, sat back, and smiled.

"Yes, it certainly was. Maybe next time we should try slurping — for the experience." I added a forced slurp which caused us both to chuckle. We stood to go. "Bye for now, McDermott. Enjoy your stay. I'm sure I'll see you at Mass before you leave."

"Yes, and thanks for an enjoyable evening."

After leaving the eatery, I took a long, easy walk. I realized for the first time that I wasn't feeling as resentful and jealous of McDermott as I had over the past few years. Perhaps contentment was slowly seeping into my soul like rain into the earth. *Well, almost. It was a process.* I said a silent prayer of gratitude. *Lord, hopefully, I can continue healing and be aware of Your plan for me. I know I need to replace my pride with humility, and with You all things are possible. Thanks for making me feel calm and for Your gifts of understanding, mercy, and love.*

CHAPTER 17

One evening, in the scorching summer heat as I was leaving work, I saw on the other side of the street an attractive young lady struggling to carry an oversize bundle. She had an oval face with high cheek bones and long, medium brown tresses reaching past her shoulders. Approaching her, I offered to help. She was oblivious of the bee resting on her green plaid dress.

She handed me two large bags. "Yes, thank you. These are cumbersome."

"What are they, if you don't mind me asking?" as I shoed away the insect.

"Fabric scraps. I asked my boss, Mr. Dennis, if I could

have them and he gladly said to take all that I needed. So, as you see, I didn't hesitate, and there are plenty more. We can't use the scraps at work, so they will be a godsend for my project."

"Oh, you too work for Mr. Dennis at the textile factory?"

"Yes, I'm a seamstress."

"Well, what a coincidence! We work at the same place. I'm a bookkeeper for Mr. Dennis."

"My goodness, really?"

"Do you like working there?"

"I do. Its steady work and a clean environment. Mr. Dennis is such a kind soul."

"Aye. I feel the same. Did you grow up in this town?"

"Yes. I was raised here in Pittsburgh, but I was born in Ireland. How about you?"

"I was born in Ireland, then came to America a few

years ago and lived in New York until recently. Some relatives live here in Pittsburgh, so I thought I'd give it a try." I held up the bags. "What do you plan to do with all these scraps?"

"I make quilts for some families who are in a hard way. My friend, Irene, mentioned a family with financial struggles she knows. They're her neighbors across town."

"That's mighty good of you."

"Not really, it's just decent. I have plenty and they don't. It's that simple. Plus, I enjoy quilting."

"Oh, okay," I answered, realizing my voice sounded high-pitched and quivery like I was nervous. *She is a pretty lass*. "How far are we going with these?"

"Only a mile straight ahead. I don't live far from work. It feels good to walk after sitting all day."

We continued walking down the sidewalk, carrying the bags of scraps. There were a few moments of silence, but it didn't feel uncomfortable. "What's your name, if I may ask?"

"You may ask all you want," she said with merriment, "but I will decide if I should answer." Her eyes, blue like twin lakes, smiled when she paused and then she answered, "Mary Colleen O'Grady."

With a cocky smile I nodded. "Good name." *And she's Irish to boot.*

"What's yours?"

"Joseph Quigley."

"Don't you own a middle name?"

"Glenn it is. Don't often need it though."

"It was given to you, so you should claim it." *She's a spunky one.*

"Absolutely," I snickered.

"Three more houses on the right is mine. It's the brick one with the front porch. I do appreciate your help, Joseph."

"Call me Joe. How long have you worked at the factory?"

"Going on two years now."

"What floor are you on?"

"Second, luckily. That way I can just throw the leftover scraps down the stairs when no one is near, instead of carrying them down. Although one day, I almost clobbered Irene on the head as she passed by. She surprised me by backtracking, and down came the material, landing on her toes."

"Yikes."

"Here we are," she told me as we turned and walked up the porch steps. "Thanks for your help, Joe."

"No trouble. Can I see you again with or without bundles?"

With a twinkle in her eye, she answered an emphatic "NO!" then grinned and said, "Just kidding. That would be nice."

"Then, how about two o'clock Saturday afternoon?"

"Yes, that will work."

"Good, I'll meet you here then." Tipping my cap, I waved goodbye. Removing my jacket, I slung it over my shoulder and strode off, my pulse racing and feeling like I could walk on air.

CHAPTER 18

Suddenly life was more interesting. Paul said he noticed me smiling at work and said, "You seem happier, Joe."

"Aye. I met an intriguing lassie the other day, and I am smitten with her. I had no idea you could be attracted to some-one after only one meeting."

"Oh yes. That will do it. It happened to me many years ago and I am glad to say marrying Anna was the best day of my life."

"Lucky lad, you are."

Saturday couldn't come soon enough. I went to pick up Mary Colleen in the early afternoon. It was a sunny, breezy summer day so we walked to the oldest community park called Bradley. She informed me it was appropriately named after a Mr. Frank Bradley who donated money to the town to be used specifically for this purpose. Once there, we sat under the row of century-old oak trees. I retrieved a little snack from my bag for us to share. Slowly munching on grapes and biscuits, we had a lively conversation.

Mary casually and happily revealed much about her childhood days. "My ancestors were half Catholic and half Protestant. Ma and Pa came to America when I was only four years old. We lived in Clare before that. My sister told me some stories she remembered from the old country. Some were funny, like the one of Ma chasing two stray dogs out of the kitchen with her broom. Another was when we took a trip into Dublin and visited Trinity College. I was apparently so mesmerized with the enormous surroundings that I wandered off in a daze. Since I was lost, I stood on a chair and plucked a string of a harp that was standing in the corner by a window repeatedly, and that's how Ma found me."

"Do you still have a fascination with harps?"

"I like hearing them but not playing them. I'm not a musician, but truly appreciate the gift of music and listening to it. I wish I could play. When I was younger, I expressed an interest in singing to my aunt, who taught voice lessons, figuring that was the next best thing. She gave me a few pointers, which I remember when I serenade around the house while cleaning. My sister, Maggie, is talented with playing the flute, but too bashful to play in front of people, although we enjoy hearing her at home."

Not caring about the time, we lazily strolled over to the magnificent gardens and circled the streaming fountains.

"Gardens are one of my favorite parts of life," Mary confided to me.

"Oh, then in our future courtships we will need to visit this and others often."

"How do you know I want future courting days with you?' she teased, blushing.

"I can see it in your sky-blue eyes."

She looked up to me with a dreamy, smiling gaze.

We then wandered slowly back to her house, hand in hand.

Bidding one another goodbye, we agreed to meet again the following weekend.

Walking home, I couldn't believe my Irish luck. I marveled at the jollity of Mary Colleen and her distinct charm.

CHAPTER 19

Assuming I would dream only of Mary, I was terribly mistaken. I couldn't believe it when I woke instead out of a terrible nightmare the next morning.

I dreamt that I won the coin toss and was assigned to a parish in a jungle. Seeing tigers, cougars, and jaguars all around me, I found it hard to even look for my church. Where were all the parishioners? My pounding heartbeat thundered in my ears. I saw no humans, only treacherous animals. Hearing a roaring sound nearby, I dashed along a narrow path on my left and came out onto a large patch of sand. Catching my breath and trying to figure out what to do next, I noticed I was beginning to sink. Oh God, have mercy! *This is quicksand!* Yelling for help got me nowhere. Trying to pull myself out only made me sink quicker. When I was covered up to my chin, I knew I would be dead momentarily. That is when I shot up from sleep, sweating, confused, and gasping. I questioned myself all over again. Had the meeting with Mary been a sign that I was on the wrong path…or the right one?

Feeling so distressed, I prayed. *Lord, how could I have that dream? I thought I accepted my loss. I am sorry I lost, yet I feel it is Your will for me. I know it must be for a reason, whatever that is, so I am trying to go forward. Am I wrong, though? I trust in You to guide me.* I opened my Bible and began reading the Psalms. Sleep came shortly after.

The following Saturday, when Mary and I visited her favorite place, we were standing in front of the yellow daylilies and red cornflowers when she said, "These are breathtaking."

"Yes, and so are you, Mary. May I kiss you?"

"Plant one here on my darkest freckle," she said pointing to her left cheek, giggling. Then her head turned. Her chin raised to my chest. Her radiant face told me yes and I kissed her on the lips, gently then passionately.

That kiss warmed my heart, and I felt an emotion stir within me that I'd never felt before, and realized love was budding within me. I hoped it would blossom in her, too.

On our walk back to her house, she asked me if I would like to join her family for supper the following Sunday.

"It's alright with your mother and father?"

"My mother always makes plenty of food, just in case she has some unexpected visitors. My father would be happy to see another man in the house. My brother took a job in New York to become a shipper, so there is just my older sister, my mother, and me. Does that answer your question?" she said in a flirty way.

"Aye, so it does."

The following Sunday I met Mary's family. They could not have been more inviting. We had a delicious dinner of lamb, potatoes, tomatoes, bread, and cake. I told her mother it reminded me of my Ma's cooking. Her father and I had good long discussions of his work at the steel mill and my work with bookkeeping. He also told me about his love of the Bodhran drums and so then I revealed my interest in the fiddle. He told me that I should bring over my instrument the next time I courted Mary so we could play music together.

As I thanked the O'Grady's for their gracious hospitality, they invited me to come back often. *How good to hear, since I was falling in love with their daughter.*

CHAPTER 20

I was sick the following week with a cold, cough, and fever. It lasted about nine or ten days. By then, it was mid-fall. Paul was sorry I was under the weather, but admitted he was glad to see me return. Work had piled up.

The next several times I courted Mary, we played chess and backgammon. One day, her sister Maggie pulled a chair over to watch. “Do you want to play either game, Maggie?” I asked.

“I like backgammon, so I’ll play the winner of that one.” While Mary and I played, I asked Maggie about her work. She went into detail about her pottery business.

“You should see her exquisite art, Joe, it’s beautiful,”

her sister complimented.

"Thanks, Mary, but I think you're prejudiced."

"No, it really is prizeworthy. You are an artist in your own right. I remember last year you received a bonus when your boss had a contest and you won." We ended our visit with her father and I entertaining her family with our music. We played well together, and I could see joy sparkling in Mary's eyes as she watched me play my fiddle.

When Christmas arrived, Mary and I were invited to my Uncle Tom and Aunt Kate's for dinner. They knew about Mary from a letter I had written in October confessing my love for her. On our way home, she told me, "I sure do like your Aunt Kate, she's indeed a lovable lady. I also enjoyed being around a large gathering. Our family is small, so it's fun listening to the children."

A few days later, we had another belated celebration with the O'Grady's. I was able to meet her brother, Richard, who was home for one week. He was one vivacious, outgoing fella, and a fun conversationalist. He informed me about his work in the shipyard, and I enlightened him of my travels. I liked that he laughed often. *It sure would be good to have him as a future brother-in-law.*

After an extended time of becoming acquainted, we were told dinner was served. Mr. O'Grady said a blessing, then we held our sherry for a toast. Mrs. O'Grady outdid herself. She served an elegant dinner of pheasant, colcannon, parsnips, glazed turnips, and bread. The table was beautifully set with her heirloom china and crystal. When I admired her pretty setting, she mentioned the embroidered linens were a gift from her mother. An overflowing bouquet of greens adorned the side buffet which held the tantalizing dessert plates. After everyone pitched in cleaning up, we all retreated into the parlor for fruitcake, trifle, fudge, and Irish coffee.

Sitting around the tree, which was decorated with popcorn and colorful homemade treasures from when the siblings were little, I felt happier than I could remember.

Richard entertained us with some jokes while Maggie reluctantly agreed to end the day with playing "Hark the Herald Angels Sing" on her flute. Mary Colleen and her mom sung along while I hummed. The candlelight glowed around us as our hearts were warmed. It was by far the best Christmas I had since I had arrived in America.

Mary Colleen O'Grady and I became engaged the first week of February, on her birthday.

I had asked Mr. O'Grady for his daughter's hand in marriage a few days earlier when Mary was in the kitchen helping her mother with the dishes.

I had pondered for a while about exactly how to propose to her. I decided to ask in the most chivalrous way—by getting down on one knee and surprising her.

Knowing how thrifty she was, I settled on a simple white, natural pearl engagement ring. After having supper again in her parent's home, Mary and I grabbed our coats and walked outside on the porch to get some fresh air. The moon shone brightly, shedding light in the area where we stood. I trembled as I retrieved the ring from my pocket, and knelt. "Mary Colleen, would you do me the honor of becoming my wife?" I asked.

With excitement caught in her throat, her "yes" was barely audible. Looking down into my eyes, she repeated, "Yes, I will." She added, "For once, I am taller than you," and giggled heartily. I stood and we engaged in a lengthy embrace. Mary gazed upon her ring, and to my delight, she said, "Pearls are my absolute favorite."

We went inside the house and announced our happy news to her parents and her sister. Congratulations and hugs were given to us both. Then, Mr. O'Grady poured us all some sherry so he could make another toast. Mary said she would send a note off to Richard to inform him.

We planned a small spring wedding. Our guests would be Aunt Kate, Uncle Tom, and their family, Mary Colleen's family, her best friend Irene, and Paul and his wife. We decided to ask her brother Richard and sister Maggie to stand for us as best man and maid of honor.

I couldn't wait to write my family with the news.

Mary's mother told us she'd help with the wedding details. I had hoped that McDermott could attend, but unfortunately, he was preparing for exams. He wished us many blessings and promised to visit when time allowed. I was disappointed but understood.

The following week we took advantage of the frigid, snowy weather by bobsledding on the hill outside her immediate neighborhood. It was a good hike away but worth every minute. Half the fun was crunching in the snow, which was knee deep on our walk. Mrs. O'Grady spoiled us by having tea and scones ready when we arrived home nearly frozen. "You kids need to thaw out. Have some tea."

"Nothing could be better right about now. Thank you," I said while plucking ice from her daughter's hair.

Mary couldn't pull off her heavy, slushy boots, so when

I yanked them off, she fell sideways, and I tilted backwards while snow dripped from her boots. We laughed so hard it made her snort which made us both laugh all the more.

After warming up, I decided it was time to head home. "Make sure you join us next week for the parish winter bazaar," Mary said, as I buttoned my coat. "It will be held in the church basement, and it's a big deal. It's their largest yearly event and lots of fun."

The bazaar was true to form. There were grab bags, sticky apples, a clown who handed out candy, and hopscotch for all the children. A ring toss game with prizes attracted the young ones too. The ladies were glad to see the white elephant table, jewelry, and baked goods. There must have been at least sixty cakes and pies for purchase. The religious table displayed rosaries, prayer books, and medals. The men enjoyed examining the table with farm tools for sale.

The live musicians played while families ate the delicious chicken dinners that were sold. The whole day was fun, and a financial help for the parish.

Before we left, Mary and I told Father Kenna, the pastor, about our wedding plan. We decided to marry the beginning of May (the month of the Blessed Mother, as Mary wished). We requested the church basement for the reception, and he happily agreed.

That night I wrote another letter to my family back home. I told them all about Mary Colleen and her terrific family. I expressed my desire for them to all be here for the wedding but knew that couldn't be. We would keep connected through the mail instead. Two months later, Aiden wrote in return, saying, *"Wishing you the best, Joe. Our whole clan is so happy for you, and we are with you and Mary in spirit. God bless you both now and always. You can expect a package from all of us in the weeks to come."*

My heart felt sad that my immediate family couldn't make it to my wedding. I was consoled, however, knowing at least my Pittsburgh relatives would be able to attend.

CHAPTER 21

Spring approached fast and our special day finally arrived. We chose a noontime Mass and ceremony. As I waited and watched my bride walk down the aisle towards me, I felt like the luckiest man alive. My knees were so weak, I hoped they wouldn't give out. But then I felt my heart sing with joy as my eyes locked with Mary's. I could see they were glowing with joy and excitement as she walked arm-in-arm with her father down the aisle.

Mr. O'Grady smiled and winked as I shook his hand, thanking him. Grasping Mary's hand, I squeezed hard. In the middle of the Mass, we exchanged our vows. But when Richard checked his pockets for the rings, he shrugged with his palms up, a shocking look on his face. "I lost them!" he whispered. Father Kenna looked as dumbfounded as me. "Just kidding," he grinned, and removed them a moment later from an inside pocket.

Then Father blessed us and the ceremony continued. The organist played the Wedding March, Gloria, Ave Maria, and Ode to Joy. The music sounded as if it came straight from heaven. We heard my youngest cousins gasp in awe as we proceeded down the aisle together as man and wife. This was their first experience at a wedding. One of them even reached out to touch Mary's knee-length, two-tiered white veil as we passed by. When we entered the vestibule, I told Mary, "You look stunning. I love you."

"You're not bad looking yourself," she softly answered, with a twinkle in her eye and a wide smile. "I love you, too."

Mary's parents had outdone themselves when it came to the reception. The banquet tables were heaped with a variety of meats, cheeses, and side dishes, and waiters refilled wine glasses so they were never empty. Dancing and singing went on for hours and everyone joined in, performing all sorts of jigs and waltzes. Guests showed off their talent with no hesitation and even the little ones swung around the room showing off their dance moves.

The room looked like an indoor garden, lavished with a multitude of spring flowers—hyacinths, dahlias, azaleas, forsythias, peonies, and primrose. Their fragrances combined to create a sweet aroma that filled the room. I did a double take as I spotted Liam dancing with Irene. *Hmmm, who knows where that might lead?* Then I overheard Molly compliment Mary. "Your gown is beautifully elegant. I especially like the floral lace overtop the satin. You look lovely.

Mr. and Mrs. O'Grady came to congratulate me. "We could not have asked for a finer, nobler son-in-law, Joe," Mr. O'Grady said, shaking my hand and then giving me a slap on the back.

"Thank you. I'm grateful to be your daughter's husband

and a member of your family."

In the middle of all the festivity, our carriage waited to take us to a small borough outside Pittsburgh for a long-awaited, three-day honeymoon, thanks to Uncle Tom and Aunt Kate. We climbed inside and began talking about our dreams as our guests continued with the celebration. Arriving at a beautiful riverside cabin, we breathed in the fresh, fragrant air. Happy for the quiet time alone in such a peaceful place, we settled in, then took a hike to familiarize ourselves with the area. That is where I revealed to my wife my aspirations of owning my own grocery store.

"Joe, that sounds like a marvelous idea!" Mary beamed with delight.

"You think so?"

"Absolutely. You have experience in bookkeeping and merchandise from working at both the shoe company and our textile factory. Besides, you are brilliant and have a supportive wife." She nodded emphatically.

"I'm concerned because I still need to send McDermott the weekly check, so I don't want us to go in the hole at the beginning when the business needs to get started."

"Sweetheart, I am frugal by nature, plus I would enjoy operating a store with you. The Lord knows we certainly could use a general store in our town."

"Some men on the train mentioned the need to me, too."

At the conclusion of that decisive discussion, we tested out the settee on the porch. While the crickets and frogs entertained us with their uniquely melodious sounds, and the aroma of the pine trees wafted through, we were enchanted, watching the moon shine across the river.

The next morning Mary yelled, "Hurry up, slow poke! The ferry is about to leave."

I grabbed a biscuit to eat on our ride.

"I've never been on a boat, Joe. This should be fun!"

"Yes, I agree. Later, let's try out my fishing gear. I haven't fished since I was home with Aiden."

"Okay. I bet I can catch a larger one than you."

"We'll see, you spirited, lovely lady."

When eating our catch for supper, Mary apologized for ruining three hooks and lines by getting them tangled and ripped in the bushes.

"Better the bushes than our hair or hands," I said with a smile.

"From now on, I will leave the catching of those slippery creatures to you and the frying of them to me."

"Deal."

We spent two more glorious days strolling, talking, and enjoying nature. We luckily dodged a path that was being traveled by a family of bears. If I had missed seeing them far ahead, we might have been their dinner. Leaving the cabin, we looked forward to our new home, a small cottage we rented, which was situated not far from the O'Grady's.

A few weeks later, Mary announced the need for a little garden. "Both vegetables and flowers would be good, but we'll start with the latter. We can trade with mother's garden treasures." It didn't take long for the flowers to appear. Her favorite plant was the lavender. She would shriek with joy picking a bunch. "Oh my gosh, inhale that fragrance, its heavenly! Our red cardinal flowers and butterfly weeds are doing spectacular. They have a dual purpose, too, because they attract hummingbirds and butterflies. And our daisies, oh, they are so beautifully simple. Joe, I love this garden, almost as much as I love you." Her Irish eyes sparkled.

"Gee, glad I rank above the flowers," I said, grinning.

"Oh, silly." Mary gave me a kiss then said, "I'll wait until next year to plant some vegetables. One thing at a time."

As far as the house furnishings, they mostly came from my aunt and uncle, and Mary's parents. . . there wasn't much we needed to purchase. Mary began working on a quilt for our own bed which was from her grandmother's pattern. The Belleek tea set and china, sent from my family back home as a wedding gift, decorated our dining table.

We visited her parents every Sunday after Mass and enjoyed a family meal.

I became preoccupied with checking out locations for my store. My uncle Liam offered to help me when the time came.

CHAPTER 22

For our first Christmas together, Mary and I decided to go to midnight Mass with her parents, then spend Christmas day by ourselves. She surprised me with an oyster stew for supper along with a beef roast. “I didn’t think I could stomach the stew, so we have a roast backup in case,” she announced when setting the table. We exchanged gifts by the fireside while the dinner was heating. She was just as thrilled with the fluffy white earmuffs and matching hat as I was with a new string for my fiddle.

“I remember you said one of your strings was broken,” she said when I began to insert the new one.

“Yes, now it plays perfectly. Thank you, darling” We

tickled each other in the face with the furry hat, then had a long kiss under the mistletoe.

The next morning, I wrote a detailed letter to Aiden. I had to explain about all the blessings that had been filling my heart.

Two days later, our expected visitor arrived.

"My how good to see you, McDermott. How was your trip?" I asked, taking my old friend's coat.

"Long, but productive, and that's because I did some long-awaited reading." He turned to my wife. "Mary, I'm so glad to finally meet you. It seems you have made a new man out of our Quigley. He looks happier than I've ever seen him." I could feel my face beaming. "Mary, this poinsettia is for you—and Joe, here is something you can enjoy." He handed me a pint of Guinness.

Mary prepared a remarkable Irish supper while I led McDermott into the parlor so that we could catch up.

"How are the studies coming along?" I asked, tending to the blaze in the fireplace.

"Well, I still have two more years before I can be ordained. Some classes are tough, but what I do like are the philosophy classes. I learned that St. Thomas Aquinas linked philosophy and theology together. It's all so fascinating. There are twelve other classmates. One chap came from Germany, and the rest are from the surrounding areas. What about your work, Quigley?"

"I like what I do, and I believe I'm rather good at it."

"You certainly do look relaxed and content."

"Aye, our company is prospering nicely, and I like my co-workers too. I've gained experience with this current position as well as my former one to the point I have decided to soon open my own business."

"I'll be darned! That sounds like exciting news. What kind of business is it?"

"I plan to open a general store, rather Mary and I will work it together. This town needs one and it can be beneficial to all the residents. I'm still trying to decide where to put it. I've searched a few possibilities, but nothing is definite yet."

"So, you are planning to build your own store, not buy an existing building?"

"That's right. I want to find a piece of property and then build. I have drawn some designs for the structure, so we'll see how it goes."

"Well, Quigley, I am happy for you, buddy. Sounds like you are turning into an entrepreneur. I'll pray it takes off as you plan."

In the middle of discussing the town of Pittsburgh, Mary called us in for supper.

"Mary, you're an excellent cook, this chicken pie is delicious."

"Thank you. It's a family recipe."

"We have tasty dinners in the seminary, but they don't compare to family favorites."

While we savored the dessert of almond pudding and tea, I mentioned to McDermott an idea for tomorrow's visit. "How would you like to go to the nearby saloon and listen to some music?"

"Hmm, not a bad idea. I have another day off before I need to head back, so yes, that sounds good."

"My dear, care to join us?" I asked.

"Thanks, but no. I told Maggie I would come over and see her new pottery she's making."

Mary filled McDermott in on her sister's work as a potter. After that, he thanked us both for a fun day. He then said to me, "Joe, you are one lucky fella to have such a lovely wife, cozy home, and a booming business on the horizon."

"Aye, I am grateful to God for my blessings, especially Mary. Ok, I will meet you at Queen of Peace rectory tomorrow afternoon. Good night."

"Good night, and thanks again." After we closed the front door, I said to Mary, "You know what, my intuition tells me that McDermott is now at ease and not feeling guilty any-more about winning the toss."

"Glad to hear it, sweetheart. He couldn't have won to a better person. I have to confess that I am glad you lost, or I would not be standing here admiring the most wonderful man on this planet." She wrapped her arms around my waist and nuzzled against my neck.

CHAPTER 23

The following spring, I had decided to build my store on a lot for sale between the railroad station and our church. Centrally located, it would attract customers from all directions. One plan after another fell into place. Starting the physical work was exciting as well as motivating. Every free moment, friends, relatives, and I would gather together and labor for as long as time permitted. By the end of autumn, the results looked rather promising. I wanted to make it large enough to hold all the goods we needed to sell. Also, I needed to make sure it could last a lifetime, so I decided to construct the outside with stone from the local quarry.

We built one large main area, and a room on the side to

hold surplus goods. A tricky part was dividing up the shelf space inside because some merchandise required more height than others. Liam made me a cart to hold flour sacks and a cabinet to house the sewing notions.

It was a challenge for us to find some of the items we wanted to sell in our store. We heard of some needs from our neighbors and searched for some specialty goods as well as necessities. Staples and first aid were a must, and of course, we had to include gift items and treats for the young and young at heart. With hard work, determination, and perseverance, it all came together and soon the store was filled with groceries, dried goods, clothing, shoes, cleaning supplies, toiletries, and even magazines and candy.

Mary and her sister worked diligently on decorating the inside. They had a flair for making the place look attractive and inviting. Seasonal flowers were placed at the entranceway. The windows displayed the enticing wares for both men and women, such as hats, boots, and capes. Baskets, canisters, mason jars, and buckets all held a variety of provisions. Barrels of sugar and spuds were among the most sought-after items. They all were placed alongside the houseware items, oils, candles, staples, and gifts. Mary and Maggie made the presentation neat and tidy. They housed the medicines, soaps, books, and magazines apart from the groceries. The front counter was designed for candy and baked goods and toys. The fabrics and farm equipment had their own corners.

By summer of the following year, our dream store, which we simply named “Quigley’s,” was well stocked and ready to open. Mr. Dennis understood when we both told him we needed to resign in order to open our own business.

Even with all the new expenses, I never missed sending McDermott his weekly checks. We just lived frugally for several years. Mary Colleen never complained about cutting corners. She was as thrifty as she was beautiful.

After a few months’ experience as a store owner, I realized the shop was becoming a social gathering for the community. Therefore, I added a table and chairs for checker players and visiting. Postmaster was a new unofficial title given me too. I sometimes needed to make trips into the large cities for supplies. On one occasion, when in New York, I stopped in to see my old friend, William. We had a good four-hour reunion that day.

As time progressed, I bought a house with a large yard. Mary's garden was her passion, yet she considered her first priority being a shop co-owner. We both took care of the ledger book. She saw what needed replacing before I did. "I couldn't run this business without you dear," I said to her one day, as I hunched over the desk, tired as could be.

"Sure you could. It just wouldn't be as classy," she teased with smiling eyes and a kiss. "Let's go in the house and sit with some tea and scones. I made them this morning, so they are good and fresh. You look tired, so you need to rest a bit."

"Cheers to you, my dear." I said as I raised my teacup. "I figured I only have two more payments to send to McDermott. Then that debt will be finished. Isn't that good news?"

"It most certainly is. You deserve a high place in heaven for being such a loyal friend helping him acquire his vocation sweetheart. I have good news myself."

"What's that?"

"You are going to be a father, too, only in a different way."

It took a few seconds for Mary's words to sink in. "Wow, really? We're going to be parents? Goodness, that is happy news!" I stood up, picked up my precious wife and kissed her. "Now, we need to cheer our little angel." "Slainte, good health little one," we said together.

After that happy revelation, I made sure Mary didn't do anything strenuous. "You need to rest dear," I would tell her before I left for the store.

"Don't worry about me Joe, I will be just fine. Our Blessed Mother must have had a harder life than I, and she did well. That goes for our own mothers too."

"You always see the bright side of everything Mary, I love that about you."

"There's no stopping me, Joe, I do enjoy the work in our store, I really do."

"Ok, but just take it easy, please."

I hired a customer to clean the store to keep Mary from doing it. He owed me money at the time, so we decided that would be a good tradeoff. As it turned out, he kept on for three more years, since money was tight for him. A few weeks later, I hired another customer to do heavy hauling of goods so I could spend the time helping Mary in the house with preparing a nursery. As our business thrived, I was able to keep him on, too. His name was Samuel, and he proved to be a hard worker.

There was plenty of paperwork that demanded my attention. Life was full and I was grateful for all of the preparation I had gained by working for Mr. Murphy and Mr. Dennis. *So glad, Lord, that you prepared me for where I am now.*

I needed to travel for supplies, and Mary was getting closer to her due date. I asked Liam to check in on Mary to see if she needed any help with anything. After Liam readily agreed to my request, he hesitated, then said, "Joe, there's something I've been meaning to talk to you about. Irene and I have been smitten with each other since the wedding. I have been moving slow with a proposal, but I think it will come soon."

"Liam, that's happy news! I'm glad for you. She's a lucky girl. I must admit, Mary and I suspected just that."

"When the time comes, I'd like for you to be my best man."

"Sure Liam, I'd be honored."

We both went back to work with smiles on our faces. Life was full of surprises.

CHAPTER 24

Before we knew it, the birth of our first child was upon us. Luckily, I made it back from my trip in time, although I wasn't really needed for anything. Mary's mother and sister were continually present waiting to assist. Irene wanted to be included in the excitement as well. She told me to go over and visit Liam while she and the O'Grady ladies did their part.

Joseph Glenn Quigley, Jr. was born many hours later. He was a healthy baby, thank the Lord, and seemed to possess the qualities of his mother, happy, aware, and curious. He resembled my father in looks with his dark hair and features. We asked Richard and Maggie to be his godparents.

We were the talk of the town for a few weeks. Relatives, friends, and customers were generous with bringing over food and baby clothes. Mrs. O'Grady cooked for us, and visitors came and went. When things settled down, we began a new routine. I went off to the store and Mary took care of the baby.

I came home from work one day and saw Mary gazing out the window. Cradling the baby, I heard her say to him, "As gorgeous as our garden is, you, my little Joseph, are way more beautiful."

Lord, what a moment! Mary's love is deeper than my anger and jealousy of the coin toss. Thank You, God. Your healing is happening within me. "How's my little family doing?" I announced walking closer to their chair.

"We have had a lovely day dear. The doctor checked the baby and said he is doing perfectly fine. Mother made us lamb pie and cake for supper and, I think our baby would like to see our store."

"Do you really?" I looked down at my son's cherubic

face and thought of my desk, messy with paperwork, the store cluttered with goods, people hanging around on the porch, mostly folks I knew, but a few of them strangers. Suddenly I felt protective. "I think we should wait until he's a little older."

"Okay, you're right. Let's wait until tomorrow, then he shall be a day older."

I couldn't help but laugh, feeling my needless anxiety melt away. I kissed my witty wife. "Sure, tomorrow is good," I said, still shaking my head grinning.

A week later, I found a letter sitting on the kitchen table. I knew it had to be from home and I tore it open, excited to read it.

"*My dear brother, hope this finds you in good health. I miss you, Joe. How are your new business plans coming along? I applaud you for wanting to open your own store. That's amazing news, Joe. We all can't wait to hear how it all unravels. You are most industrious.*

John and Shane, our twin brothers, are now taller than

me. John has taken up the accordion. He does really well with it, too. Shane enjoys hunting. He brought us home a few ducks last week for dinner and they were delicious. Patrick is still itching to go abroad. Ma and Aunt Sharon have organized a group of ladies at church to take turns visiting the sick in the parish and taking meals.

Pa is slowing down. He said his age is creeping up on him. The twins have been helping me with the farm more now to relieve him. Well, not much more to say. Look forward to hearing from you. Stay well. Give Mary our love. Your brother, Aiden

A few days later, Liam came over to the store to tell me his marriage plans. "Joe, since Irene's parents live in Foxburg and don't like to travel, we decided to venture there for our wedding. It shouldn't take more than a day to get there. That way, her parents don't have to miss the wedding. Michael and Owen said they can do my part in helping Pa while I'm gone. My neighbor will come over to milk the cows so that will be a big help. Therefore buddy, I will have to ask her brother to stand for me, sorry for the change.

"Of course, I understand perfectly. I answered.

"We wanted you and Mary to be there, too, but I know with the baby and the store, it would be too hard for you to take the time and travel."

"You're right about that, but we can celebrate when you get back."

"Good. We'll look forward to that. I'm beginning to feel nervous about getting married, but in a happy way. Is that normal?" He asked as he paced back and forth in front of me raising his arms in wonderment.

"Yes, absolutely it is. Liam, relax. You'll be fine." I slapped him on his shoulder.

"I guess because I'm older, it's a little harder to de-cide."

"Once it's over, you'll feel relieved. Why did she move here from Foxburg anyway?"

"For her job. There were no textile industries there and she enjoys working with fabric.

"Aye. When do you plan to go?"

"Next week, after I get the stable ready for our new calf. He should be born soon after we return."

"Good luck, Liam, I'm sure everything will work out well, the way God wants it to." I felt like I was telling myself this, too, feeling a bit wistful and nostalgic. I would miss being at Liam's wedding, but knew it was for the best.

CHAPTER 25

When Joe Jr. turned two years old, Mary announced that he was going to be a big brother. We were at supper when she broke the happy news. I had just taken a drink of milk which then got sprayed over my plate. "Goodness, that's terrific." I sputtered, catching my breath. "Maybe you should reveal exciting news when I don't have a mouthful of food or drink." Chuckling, my wife agreed.

As our business continued to thrive, I needed to hire someone to help with the customers. I was busy purchasing goods, traveling, and trying to decrease the piles of paperwork. I also figured I might need to be home more hours when our second child arrived. We heard at church that a parishioner, named Lucy Lankin, was looking for work. She started helping us and caught on fast when Mary explained her duties. Being outgoing, she and the customers developed a good rapport. She and Mary became fast friends.

Several months later, when baby Marita was born, Lucy came over to the house often after work to help Mary. She quickly became acquainted with the O'Grady's. She enjoyed visiting with Mary's mother over tea while they both did their knitting. She was a good bit older than us and had a son of her own. "He decided to go out west to look for gold. That's why I enjoy being around little children," she told us one afternoon after playing with little Joseph. "I like to think of your Joseph and Marita as my adopted grandchildren, since I highly doubt I will have any of my own."

A year later, Irene and Liam had their first child. Mary and Irene were so glad that their children had each other for cousins. "One big happy family," the mothers would often say.

Some news from the town folk and regular customers

led me to think about adding a dimension to my business. I heard there were some surrounding communities who lacked a fully-equipped store in their area, and had no transportation to mine. Therefore, I was inspired to begin operating as a green-grocer who delivered fresh produce among other items to these people. I painted on one of my two wagons the sign, "Quigley's Greengrocer." These weekly trips caused me to work extra hours. It became a gratifying job because the recipients expressed such appreciation, but after months of adding this extra work, Mary noticed how fatigued I had become. One morning at breakfast she said to me, "Joe, you need to ask your assistant Samuel to take over the deliveries. I'm worried about your health."

"I was thinking the same thing," I told her. "He said to me that he likes working with us and has more time if we needed to increase his hours."

"Good then, that's settled. Now, it's time for me to hear you play your fiddle."

"Really?"

"Yes. You haven't taken time to relax with that for ages. Please play, Mr. Quigley," she lovingly ordered, settling down on our sofa. "I'll pretend we are at the grand theatre."

My muscles instantly relaxed as I let out a huge breath. "My, Mrs. Quigley, you offer such excellent advice," I happily answered.

The next evening, little Joe spied my fiddle sitting on the parlor table. He picked it up and began strumming. "I can play music, Papa," he told me.

"Yes, you can, but I think we need to get you an instrument for your size." I gently took it from him. Minutes later, he began banging on the pots and pans.

The greengrocer addition went well. We received much feedback from grateful customers. Two more years rolled by with more orders and more deliveries. *What an expansion, thank You, Lord.*

When I happened to have a little break time from work, I wrote a long, overdue letter to Aiden. It contained lots of news about my business and the children. I caught him up to date with everything.

A short while later, McDermott wrote to say he was ordained, and that he was going to take a short vacation in Pennsylvania before he was to begin his first assignment. He asked if he could visit his "friend and enabler" while he was in the area.

We happily greeted Father McDermott who looked like quite the mature man. "Failte!" I saluted him, which meant "welcome" in Irish. I realized my anxiety and resentment over seeing him had finally disappeared through the goodness of God. I remarked how well and settled he appeared.

"I do say so for you, too," he answered. "It's good to see you."

"Well Jim, now that you're a priest, where is the bishop going to place you?"

"I've been assigned to a parish in Vermont. So, I was thinking that since it's so mountainous, perhaps I need to buy some hiking boots. I've been told it's a growing parish with energetic parishioners. So, wish me luck."

"It just so happens we sell a good supply of boots in our store. You can check them over and take a pair on the house."

"My gracious, Quigley, your generosity is astounding. I do appreciate that."

Over supper we discussed the occupations in Vermont and life in general. "Many of the jobs in demand are carpenters, blacksmiths, and brick masons. Of course, like most places, farmers are always busy. Also, the marble business is blooming in some of the towns. Mary, again your dinner is superb. Tell me about your store, Quigley."

I filled McDermott in on all the newest happenings. When we adjourned to the parlor for sweets and more tea, little Joe and Marita lost their shyness with our guest. Before we knew it, we all were rolling the ball back and forth to each other. "You are blessed to have such a beautiful family, Joe." Little Marita cocked her head with a mischievous look in her eyes and gave us all a sunshine smile as she teased us with holding the ball against her chest. Her competitive brother who played more seriously, scolded her. "Marita, you can't hog it, throw it to someone." She frowned at him and tossed it to our guest.

"Don't I know it." I felt tears of joy spring to my eyes.

"What's your favorite game, little Joe?" McDermott playfully tousled my son's dark curls.

"I have lots of favorites… hide and seek, baseball, dominoes, and playing Mass and store."

"I like your selections, son. They all sound fun indeed."

McDermott said it was time for him to go as Mary rounded up the children to begin their bedtime routine. "Well, Joe, whenever you and Mary care to travel to Vermont, please come in to visit me. I better be going now. You're the best friend anyone could have. I shall always be grateful to you for your kind spirit. I offered my first Mass up for you, Joe. It's the most fitting gift I could think of."

"Before you leave, can you give us and our home a blessing?"

"Absolutely."

The children mimicked Jim as he gestured and prayed.

As we shook hands afterwards, I wished McDermott blessings on his new path. "Write when you can."

CHAPTER 26

Baby number three was born the morning after a frigid night's downpour which made the ice-covered tree limbs sparkle in the sun like they were covered with diamonds. Since Mary's parents were both deceased by then, Maggie and Irene were at Mary's bedside along with a mid-wife. They worked together to deliver our little daughter Monica. However, soon after her birth, tragedy struck.

Mary started to hemorrhage and had a high fever. The women did everything they knew to try to comfort her until the doctor arrived, but by the time he got to our home, it was too late. As I kissed my precious, beloved wife and prayed over her, she journeyed to heaven.

Excruciating pain flooded me, I felt like I was suffocating, and could barely breathe. *Oh, God no, I can't bear this!* I fell into the nearest chair, shaking all over.

The baby's cry brought me out of my trance and my own weeping. The children needed my attention. I held the two older ones while Maggie took the baby. My grief and mourning overwhelmed me. But somehow, a few days later, through His grace only, I once again accepted my cross. Staggering forward with no energy, I blindly fulfilled routines. Lucy and Sam took over the store in those first few days. God heals the broken hearted. Life goes on.

Business had to continue, and our children kept growing. I had to make some decisions. Maggie knew of my dilemma about needing help with the children. Before I asked her, she kindly offered. "Joe, you need help taking care of the children. I am their aunt and since Mother and Dad are not here, I am willing to care for my nephew and nieces."

"Maggie, that is most generous, but you have your pottery business. I don't want you to sacrifice that. You enjoy it."

"My family is more important, Joe. The children and I get along so well. I would be happy to do what I can. I know I can't take Mary's place, but I will do my best with helping you raise your family. Also, Lucy visits often, so she can help me when she comes over. When my arm gets tired of throwing the ball for little Joe, I'll give that job to her," she said with a giggle. I'll warn you though, that my cooking will not begin to compare to dear Mary's, but I'll do my best."

After that discussion, I had to think if there was another solution for Maggie's sake. I thought and thought of other options but came up with nothing. A few days later I told Maggie, "You are a true blessing. I humbly accept your offer and thank you immensely. I know Mary is so pleased with your kindness. You don't need to sell your house. With Sam and Lucy's help, I don't need to leave for the store till mid-morning. That way, you can have a reprieve and some quiet, at least part of the day. As far as your cooking goes, I promise, I will appreciate every bite. You can soon give Marita some tips."

That night I prayed a psalm of thanksgiving over and over for her kindness and help, and then with a sad heart, a psalm of lamenting came from my lips.

It was difficult telling Aiden about Mary. My family sent all sorts of condolences and many Mass offerings.

Liam and Irene came to visit often, too. They had always been a comfort and good support and were no less now. I told them of the morning soon after Mary died, when I was so cranky and snapped at Lucy for no reason. And then, with Sam, I kicked over a pile of boxed screws and nails that he had just lined up. "I felt terrible afterwards and apologized."

"I'm sure they understood, Joe, they know you were heartbroken," Liam said. "Don't worry." As months progressed, little Joe, (who wanted us to drop the "little") and Marita, began helping with small tasks at home and in the store. They played with some of the children who came in with their parents.

As they grew a few years older, we had big celebrations

with them receiving the sacraments of Penance and Holy Communion. When he grew into his teen years, Joe Jr. mentioned to me about wanting to become a priest. My heart burst with joy upon hearing his words. Two years later, Marita said she desired to become a sister of charity. That announcement made my heart swell with gladness again, too.

I sang praise to God for these two vocations. *Lord, was this Your plan all along? Is this why You had me lose the coin toss, so You could be glorified by more than one vocation?*

It occurred to me to write to McDermott to inform him of this spectacular news. I invited him to the ordination whenever it would happen. Weeks later, he replied with great enthusiasm.

When Joe was only one week away from ordination, we had unexpected company. Hearing a heavy knock, I opened the door and gasped with disbelief. I jerked backwards, hitting my head on the doorframe. My mouth fell wide open in shock as I stared hard at our guests. I was speechless.

They spoke first. “You didn’t think we would miss our nephew’s ordination, did you?” Aiden laughed loudly and gave me a big tight hug.

Patrick followed. “Hi, big brother!”

“Come in, come in,” I finally managed to say to my brothers. “Wow! Boy, am I happy to see you! A joyous day indeed!” I grabbed their arms.

“We wanted to surprise you, Joe.”

“You more than succeeded,” I said while holding my chest. “I never imagined this would ever happen.”

“Well, I have been wanting to come to America ever since you left home, Joe,” Pat said.

“And a year ago, I started thinking about joining him so I could visit you.” Aiden added. “We saved up every bit of money we could, and the twins offered to take over our work, so here we are.”

“How long can you stay?”

"Well buddy, if I'm not a bother, I figured on two weeks. Then I need to get back home to make sure Shane and John are still holding down the fort."

"You kidding? You're welcome to stay forever. What about you Pat?"

"I checked out some jobs in demand in New York, and the one I'm interested in is becoming a telegraph operator. So, I will have to leave right after the ordination. If I acquire that position, then you and I will be close enough to visit."

"That sounds like an interesting job, Pat. Hope you get it. New York is bustling, unlike the quietness here.

The sun beamed through the kitchen window as it did in my heart while I fixed my brothers some lemonade. We all sat down in my living room." Take the comfy chair, Pat, and lay down on the sofa, Aiden. I'm sure you fellows are exhausted."

"Not really. Our adrenaline has set in from the excitement of seeing you."

"Ok, then tell me, how was your voyage, besides being long?"

"Not as bad as we expected," Pat said. "We met some interesting people. One was a doctor from Clare. He initiated daily card games with us and the others who felt like engaging, and there were lots of children on board. We heard from the deck hands and even some of the officers that the passengers have been more congenial than in the past decade. However, we were grateful to finally arrive here."

Aiden started talking about home. "Pa's health is failing, and Ma is worried about him. He's thinking about selling off one half of the property and livestock to make things an easier go. Uncle Robert is considering buying it so he and Aunt Sharon could build a small cottage and be within walking distance of Ma and Pa."

"That sounds like a fine plan. It would be ideal for all four of them."

In the middle of talking, Monica came out of the

kitchen to meet her uncles. After all the introductions were made, she said, "I just cooked a magnificent supper; pork roast, colcannon, and lemon pudding."

When compliments were extended to the young chef, Monica gave credit to her instructor, Aunt Maggie.

"How is Maggie doing, Joe?" inquired Aiden.

"Well, now that the children are older and self-sufficient, she has been spending most of the time at her home. She rides to Mass with us and spends the rest of the day here. She taught Monica the skill of pottery, and Marita took up the flute from her influence. Her brother, Richard, comes monthly to visit her since their folks are deceased. She and Irene visit frequently with each other too."

"How is Marita doing in the convent? We think of her often and wish we could be here when she takes her vows. What order did you say she is entering?"

"The Sisters of Charity. She's not far from here, in Seton Hill."

"Oh right. Two vocations in this family. You are truly blessed, Joe. It's something how life works out. We were so sad for you when you lost the coin toss many years ago, and now two of your children are fulfilling the same dream you had. You must be overjoyed."

"Yes, I can't tell you how happy it makes me. I thank God each day."

After a lengthy discussion about Marita, I pulled out my fiddle and we sang until yawns became contagious. "Tomorrow, you boys can join me at the store, and I want you to meet Liam and his family."

"Can't wait," Aiden answered.

"I'm so curious to see your store and the Quigley clan," added Pat.

Monica helped me make up the guest room and it didn't take long before everyone fell asleep.

CHAPTER 27

"This is mighty impressive, Joe," Aiden exclaimed as my brothers stepped inside my store.

"You can say that again," Pat added.

Looking all around, Aiden said, "It seems like you have everything anyone would ever need."

Pat chatted with Sam and Lucy while I followed behind Aiden. When he spotted the rockers, we sat down, and I went into detail about all the ins and outs of my business.

"You've done well, Joe. Ma and Pa would be so proud. I see a few goodies Ma would like. I'll take them back for her."

"By all means. Take some souvenirs for yourself, too."

Sam interrupted our visit by handing me a letter. “This just arrived yesterday, boss.”

“Thanks, Sam.” I opened it and read that McDermott was looking forward to coming to Joe’s ordination. “Fantastic!” I was so surprised I didn’t realize I’d uttered the words aloud.

“What’s that about?” inquired Aiden.

I proceeded to tell him about inviting McDermott to the ordination. “He said he would meet us at the church.”

“Oh good, then we can meet him too.” Aiden seemed genuinely thrilled. My younger brother had heard of my triumphs and tragedies where my friend McDermott was concerned, before and after that fateful coin toss on the ship ride to America.

“Yes, we are good friends now. I have no animosity toward him, thank the Lord. I am glad you and Pat can meet him.”

After leaving the store, I took the boys for a ride in my wagon. We went to visit Liam and Irene. "Well, well, how good it is to see you Aiden and Pat! Joe speaks of you often." When conversations led from one topic to another, Irene put together a scrumptious late lunch for us all. Their four children joined in for a short time. At dusk we headed home. Both the brothers said how pleased they were to finally meet some distant relatives.

Two days later, we all headed to the train station to travel to New Jersey. It took one full day to arrive, and we then had to hail down a carriage to reach Immaculate Conception Seminary.

My son's big day came with all the excitement and joy my heart could hold. There were sixteen other men being ordained at that time. What a glorious day in my life to witness my son becoming a priest. Mary Colleen would have been thrilled.

It was good to have my brothers, Monica, Maggie,

Liam, and McDermott attend with me. Marita was unable to accompany us because she was preparing for her vocation, but said she was with us in spirit. I prayed in thanksgiving for this special and blessed occasion.

After the Mass of Ordination was over, we celebrated at a popular saloon in the area. Joe Jr. told us at supper that he could return home for a little vacation before he began his assigned work at St. Anastasia parish in Teaneck, New Jersey.

During dinner, McDermott regaled some of our funny stories from our ship excursion and told my family about how much he appreciated my friendship. "Your dad, your brother, your friend…Joe, he's one in a million. The day of our coin toss is still most vivid in my mind. I don't know of any man who would sacrifice his dream like he did. I will be forever grateful."

"No hard feelings, McDermott." I held back tears of gratitude that started to fall. "God saw to it that I was actually the winner thanks to my kids." I tried to lighten the moment.

"Maybe we should have another toss to see who will eat the dessert that Maggie doesn't want." Laughter was shared at our celebration table. We all spent the night in a nearby hotel before heading home the next day.

Pat and McDermott left to travel north as the rest of us left to go west to Pittsburgh. The train ride was filled with happy conversation. Joe Jr. and Aiden became acquainted and had much discussion about churches in Ireland and those here in America.

"Oh, by the way Joe, did your dad tell you about the apparition in Knock?" Uncle Aiden asked.

"Yes, but I don't remember all the details."

"It happened a few years ago, in August of '79, and it was magnificent! There were people of all ages, young and old, who testified to the miracle by the side of a chapel. Our Lady was in the middle of St. Joseph and St. John. Mayo and all of Ireland were truly blessed with that event. To this day, pilgrims attend the site for healing in commemoration of

Mother Mary's appearance."

"Did you and your family go?"

"You bet! It's not that far from home, so we all went together after Mass one Sunday and then I took Ma over a second time one afternoon. It gave us a great feeling of peace to be there. I heard others say it enlightened their faith.

The next day, Monica and I headed off to work while my son and brother slept. She enjoyed teaching at the rural school five miles away and I needed to check out the latest deliveries. It was such a delight to see Joe and Aiden at home when I returned from work. They surprised us by having supper ready. "You'll spoil us," I said while chomping my last bite.

"We wanted to make ourselves useful," Aiden answered.

"And this is a good break from academics," Joe added.

Monica invited us to join her and her fiancé, Emmett,

on the tennis court before our company left.

"Since when did you learn tennis?" her brother asked.

"Since Emmett taught me last year. It's so fun and invigorating. He teaches twice a week after work during the summer."

"What's his line of work?" Joe asked.

"He's an engineer for the Pittsburgh Steel Company."

"Well, Monica, thanks but I think since I'm here for such a short time, your dad and I will just visit while you youngsters play," Aiden said. We three gents savored our time with each other before Aiden had to return home and Joe had to begin his pastoral duties at St. Anastasia Church. It felt good to catch up and just enjoy our chance to be together. I made an appearance at the store, but until our company left, I was mostly at home with them.

When Monica asked her brother to marry her and Emmett, he enthusiastically agreed. "Sure sis, your wedding will be my first marriage I can officiate. How about confession? Want me to hear it?" he asked, teasing her.

"In your dreams, big brother," she responded, giving him a playful shove.

Our treasured moments ended when I waved goodbye to Aiden as he hopped into the carriage which took him to New York to board his steamer to the green pastures of home. "Godspeed, my brother and best friend," I said softly, my heart aching in my chest. I recalled decades ago when it was me leaving in the opposite direction. *What a long, long time ago.*

Joe spent some hours helping me in the store conversing with all the customers. They were happy to see him look so mature and content. He remarked how business had grown since he went away to the seminary. When it was time for him to leave, his hug and handshake spoke volumes. "God bless you, dear son. Enjoy the new chapter in your life," I told him, choking back tears for the second time that day.

"Thanks Pop, thanks for everything. See you in a few months at Mon's wedding."

CHAPTER 28

The next morning, I did some deep reflecting and recalled all my unexpected blessings. I then wandered down to the store, not wanting to take advantage of Sam and Lucy's kindness filling in while I was gone. The fragrance of the sweet air following the night rain, caused me again to praise God, this time for simple joys.

I thanked Lucy and Sam for taking good care of the place. They showed me a new line of straw hats that arrived and said how popular the sewing notions had been. They also pointed to the extra amount of medicines that we ordered.

I rummaged through the mail and saw a letter from Marita. It read, "*Hello, Papa. I am doing very well and I'm so happy here. I'm excited to make my final vows in just another year. My class and I are helping in the St. Joseph Academy for girls. But then, next year, when I make my perpetual profession, Sister Anina told me that I will no doubt work in the Charity Hospital of Pittsburgh. I am so looking forward to that! Sister Petranella is an excellent cook. She has clever ways of using vegetables. Most of the other girls here are friendly and pleasant. I have finally gotten used to waking at the crack of dawn. One of my friends, a novice, kept falling back to sleep the other day and missed prayer and breakfast. I told her the more we do it, the easier it gets. Have to go now. Oh, one more thing. I have decided to take my religious name as Sister Mary Joseph, after mom and you. Tell everyone I send my love. Blessings to you, Papa. — Marita."*

I prayed silently, my heart full of thanks. *It's gratifying, Lord, to read Marita's letter. Now that the children are settled, or nearly so, in their own vocations, and my dear Mary Colleen is with You in heaven, I am thinking hard about selling my store and becoming a Carmelite brother. Please let me know if this idea is from You or whether it's another one of my own thoughts like when I was young. Amen.*

I folded my daughter's letter and placed it in my pocket. Feeling ravished, I invited Sam and Lucy to have lunch with me. We opened some cans and cooked on the burner in the back room. Lucy made it more appealing by adding a few spices and some slices of meat.

"I heard from my son," she volunteered. "He has had some luck with finding a few pieces of gold, but more than that, he has found a wife. So now, I have a daughter-in-law."

"Happy news Lucy!" I answered.

"It was worth the trip," Sam added.

"Yes, I am glad for him. Hope they come back East, though. I miss him badly."

"If not, you should go West," I told her, and Sam agreed.

"You both think so? Hmmm. Maybe I will. I'll give it

some thought."

"Since it is a perfect spring day, and we don't have any customers now, let's clean up and leave a little early to enjoy the outdoors."

"I love this time of year," Sam said. "I've already started planting my garden."

"Aye. Gardening was Mary's hobby too. See you to-morrow, folks."

As I strolled around my property, then went to the park, I prayed to be infused with God's wisdom about the burning desire to become a Carmelite brother.

Three weeks later, Emmett had dinner with Monica and me. He mentioned that one of his co-workers had a friend in Boston who worked in sales and was looking to buy his own business. "He was tired of being an employee and wanted to become an employer."

I suddenly felt a fast pulse and inner excitement. "Is

that so?" I asked.

"Yeah, why, Mr. Quigley, do you know someone my friend's buddy could talk with?"

"I do indeed. Me."

"YOU Papa?" Monica squealed, while giving me a dazed look.

"Yes. You see. I have been thinking about becoming a Carmelite brother now that you children are grown. If I can find a buyer for my store, then it should work out."

"Gosh, that's a surprise Papa, although I know you will make a fine brother.

"Yes, you certainly will, Emmett agreed. We're happy for you."

"I have contacted the order and have been accepted, even though I will be older than most other men. However, it's contingent on being able to sell the store. Therefore, I will be most pleased to speak with the gentleman you mentioned, Emmett."

"Well, tomorrow at work I will relay what you said to my friend."

"Thank you. I believe it is God's grace working through this opportunity.

"Have you told Joe or Marita?"

"Not yet. I wanted to make sure it would work out first, and now, it seems it will. God is so good."

"Yes, He is." Monica answered, as she moved closer to Emmett, held his hand, and beamed.

Several days later, I received a telegraph from a Mr. Eugene Doyle from Boston, Massachusetts. He planned to come to Pittsburgh by train the following week to talk with me about buying my store. His message gave me encouragement, so I contacted Joe and Marita to inform them of my decision. Like their sister, they too were surprised but happy for me.

Mr. Doyle was middle aged, with a short beard on his

long face. His eyes were bright with excitement at the prospect of buying my store. We talked for a good while at home, then I took him over to the store to show him around. He met Lucy and Sam. I told him that part of the deal was to have Sam continue if he wanted since he knew the routine and was with me for years. Lucy had told me earlier that she had decided to travel to California to live with her son and his wife.

"I am most impressed, Mr. Quigley, with what I see," Mr. Doyle told me after touring the store. To tell you the truth, it is far better than I imagined. I would very much like to buy this store of yours, and yes, if Sam wants to stay on with me, I would be fortunate to have him do so. It would be a big benefit to me, so I will be glad to give him a fat bonus."

Sam grinned and rolled his eyes.

After explaining details and answering a number of questions, we shook hands and signed papers. It was over. *Praise God!*

Weeks later, Liam accompanied me to the monastery.

We had a good, long talk. We met Brothers Colin and Matthew as we entered the foyer. They greeted us warmly and tried to convince Liam to stay for supper. He thanked them but said he needed to head home. I was taken on a tour and met some other brothers. They showed me my room and I unpacked.

Soon supper was served, and I was given a formal welcome. This congenial group gave me a feeling of connectedness. I felt like I belonged. *I was home again.*

As I fell off to sleep, I prayed, *Thank You God, for leading me to where You want me to be." Happy the man who makes the Lord his trust."*

THE END

AMDG

Not my will, but Yours be done."

Luke 22:42

GROUP REFLECTION QUESTIONS

1. What in your life could cause you to trust more fully in God's plan?

2. What would you do if you lost the coin toss?

3. How long would it take you to get over the resentment of losing?

4. Would you stay friends with the winner and continue sending weekly checks like Quigley did?

5. How hard is acceptance?

6. Have you had to wait years to see pain transfer to joy?

7. Who is your favorite character in the story and why?

Printed in the USA
CPSIA information can be obtained
at www.ICGtesting.com
CBHW060234020224
3966CB00008B/121

9 798218 239138